Toshio Satou
Illustration by Nao Watanuki
W9-BKF-536
10
Suppose a Kid from the LAST DUNGEON BOONIES Moved to a Starter Town

...Huh?!
Kikyou
An odd-jobs girl.
Astounded by Lloyd's work skills!
I may have been weak back home...
but leave the cooking prep to me!

And done!
©Nao Watanuki

©Nao Watanuki
"Your profile is better than any view."
Are Lloyd and Selen on a date
to discuss a potential marriage?!

"Eh-heh-heh."
"Isn't the lake lovely, Sir Lloyd?"

Nothing like a hot bath to get girls talking! ♥

©Nao Watanuki
This hotel comes complete with an outdoor bath.

[CONTENTS]

3

Toshio Satou
Illustration by
Nao Watanuki

Suppose a Kid from the Last Dungeon Boonies Moved to a Starter Town 3

TOSHIO SATOU

Translation by Andrew Cunningham
Cover art by Nao Watanuki

Yen On
150 West 30th Street, 19th Floor
New York, NY 10001

Visit us at yenpress.com • facebook.com/yenpress • twitter.com/yenpress
yenpress.tumblr.com • instagram.com/yenpress

First Yen On Edition: September 2020

Yen On is an imprint of Yen Press, LLC.
The Yen On name and logo are trademarks of Yen Press, LLC.

The publisher is not responsible for websites (or their content) that are not owned by the publisher.

Library of Congress Cataloging-in-Publication Data
Names: Satou, Toshio, author. | Watanuki, Nao, illustrator. | Cunningham, Andrew, 1979- translator.
Title: Suppose a kid from the last dungeon boonies moved to a starter town / Toshio Satou ; illustration by Nao Watanuki ; translation by Andrew Cunningham.
Other titles: Tatoeba last dungeon maeno murano shounen ga jyoban no machi de kurasuyouna. English
Description: First Yen On edition. | New York, NY : Yen ON, 2019-
Identifiers: LCCN 2019030186 | ISBN 9781975305666 (v. 1 ; trade paperback) | ISBN 9781975306236 (v. 2 ; trade paperback) | ISBN 9781975313043 (v. 3 ; trade paperback)
Subjects: CYAC: Adventure and adventurers—Fiction. | Self-esteem—Fiction.
Classification: LCC PZ7.1.S266 Tat 2019 | DDC [Fic]—dc23
LC record available at https://lccn.loc.gov/2019030186

ISBNs: 978-1-9753-1304-3 (paperback)
978-1-9753-1305-0 (ebook)

10 9 8 7 6 5 4 3 2 1

LSC-C

Printed in the United States of America

Suppose
a Kid from the
LAST DUNGEON
BOONIES Moved
to a Starter Town

Character Profiles

Alka

Chief of the town of legend. Dotes on Lloyd as if he's her own son. Seeing Lloyd's hotel uniform may just be enough to set her off!

Marie the Witch

Disguises herself as an information broker on the East Side but is actually the princess of the Azami Kingdom. Lloyd makes her heart race for all kinds of reasons!

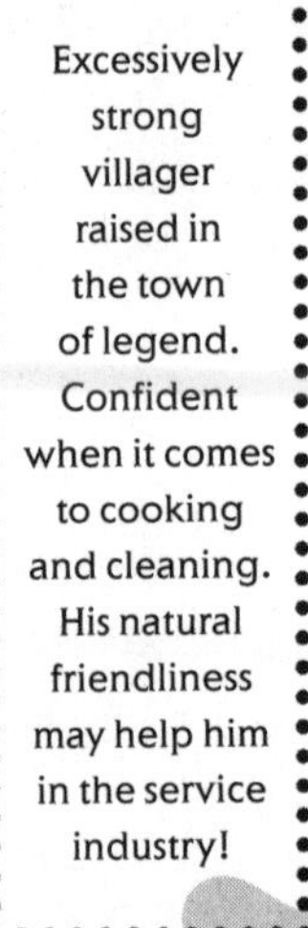

Excessively strong villager raised in the town of legend. Confident when it comes to cooking and cleaning. His natural friendliness may help him in the service industry!

Lloyd Belladonna

Allan Lidocaine

Son of a decorated noble family. Meeting Lloyd has only spread his fame.

Riho Flavin

Skilled mercenary. In it for the money. Lately seems preoccupied with Lloyd's every move.

Selen Hemein

Former Cursed Belt Princess. Devoted to Lloyd, who changed her destiny. ♥

Phyllo Quinone

A martial artist who admires Lloyd. Mena's little sister. Attends the Azami Military Academy.

Mena Quinone

A brilliant young mage. Has left Rokujo Sorcery Academy and is now involved with Lloyd's school.

Coba Lamin

Hotel owner. Retired Azami soldier. Hires Lloyd.

Shouma

A Kunlun villager. Prone to yammering about "passion." Currently traveling the world.

Threonine Lidocaine

A local lord. Allan's father. Visiting the hotel for reasons of his own.

Kikyou

An odd-jobs girl. Part of the hotel staff. Responsible for training Lloyd.

The student meal hall at the Azami Military Academy.

Teeming with youthful students chatting merrily—a quality sorely lacking in two men seated opposite each other at one table.

One of them, Colonel Chrome Molybdenum, was an instructor here.

A square-bodied man muscular down to his fingertips, he was a former member of the royal guard. Yet he was surprisingly well-versed in the art of cooking, as long as you weren't fussy about the flavor.

Across from him sat a burly bald man in his forties. His wrinkled suit said traveling businessman, but everything else about him screamed soldier. If you looked closely, you could see scars lurking between his wrinkles from years of hardship, suggesting he'd lived through the thick of it.

The students were giving the pair's table some distance, as if some shady deal was going down.

Chrome sat up straight but bowed his head.

"It's been a while, Coba."

Coba shrugged off the formality. "No need for that. I'm just a businessman now."

"You may have left the military, but you're still a respected veteran."

Coba flashed him a dry smile. "You haven't changed, at least. So? How's it going?"

"Pretty well, thanks. Found the princess, avoided having the throne snatched out from under us, doing what I can to lead the next generation."

Coba whistled, a chuckle setting his shoulders shaking. His smile seemed genuine. "Glad to hear it. Where'd you find— No, I'd better not ask. I'm an outsider now."

"Don't be ridiculous. Coba Lamin, my predecessor as head of the royal guard? I haven't forgotten how helpful the information you gathered during the crisis was."

"Ah, it was nothing special." Coba shrugged, draining his glass of water.

"How have you been, Coba? I hear you've been keeping yourself busy."

"Yeah, the hotel is finally starting to pay off. I'm running myself ragged securing supplies and personnel. Feels like I'm working harder than I ever did in the army."

Both men laughed.

"Gah-ha-ha. Doesn't matter if you're head guard or a proprietor of a hotel; if you're in charge, the work never ends. Forty-five, and I'm still learning new tricks," Coba admitted.

"Always better to be busy. I've heard people talking about Reiyoukaku. They say the hotel there is great."

"Yeah, we're pretty focused on our clients' needs, after all—"

Coba launched into a lengthy spiel about Reiyoukaku's business.

Located off the beaten path, near the mountains, the town was a former hub for lumber. Now it boasted a man-made lake and a secluded hot spring. It had a well-established reputation for natural splendor among those in the know.

But for a long time, the inns there had been for merchants and freight industry types—nothing for the upper crust or vacationing families.

So Coba had built a luxury hotel. Not to compete with the existing inns—in fact, he swore that the boost in tourism had brought more merchants through the area, and it was a win-win for everyone involved.

"The hotel's hot spring pulls its waters from the secluded one, which— Oh, listen to me, yammering away. The business life has really gone to my head."

"Hot spring, huh? I'd sure like to visit sometime."

"Oh? Then have I got an offer for you."

Coba had clearly been waiting for this. He leaned across the table with an impish grin, like a friend about to make a suggestion you should really refuse.

Chrome had seen this look on his face before and immediately began choosing his words carefully. "An offer…?"

"No need to get your guard up. I ain't trying to eat you alive here."

"Experience tells me the more you say something's gonna be fine, the more I'll suffer for it."

Coba slapped his hairless dome and made a face that said *you got me.* The gesture proved sufficiently disarming, and Chrome found it hard to stay annoyed.

"No, no, no," Coba said. "Nothing like that. I could just use some additional help around the hotel for the next holiday. We're so short-handed!"

"You want my help?"

"Yeah, you've worked as a cook before… Although, if I'm being honest, I've got a famous local lord staying and could use a few experienced guards."

"That sounds ominous."

Coba stirred the ice in his glass. It clinked around. He looked like a kid caught in a lie.

"Yeah, you see, there's been a string of incidents in the vicinity. People turning up comatose. If anything like that happened to a VIP… I'm sure it's just a minor monster, but I don't want a black mark on the hotel's name just as things are taking off."

Chrome nodded gravely. "And that's where I come in. Hmm… comatose?"

"Yeah, like the life has been drained out of them. They stay under for three days and three nights. We can't figure out if it's a monster or a human behind it. Real sinister."

It all sounded familiar to Chrome. He stroked his chin, racking his brain.

"Hmm...sounds like a treant."

"A treant? The tree-shaped monsters from fairy tales?"

"From what I've heard, they use their roots to sap the life energy from passing animals and travelers. Anyone affected is left comatose for three days and three nights...and treants are found in remote mountain regions. You say the area was once known for lumber?"

Coba slapped his head again, looking impressed.

"You sure know your stuff! Guess you ain't a teacher for nothing."

"Yeah, well...there's rumors going around about illegal treant cultivation somewhere in Azami. As a countermeasure, the government has given us all a basic briefing."

"Interesting. Glad to hear the government's on top of things. Well, if there's illegal treant cultivation going on in my neck of the woods, I definitely need your help."

Coba doubled down, but Chrome just shifted uncomfortably.

"Do I really seem like hotel staff?"

"Oh, please. I admit, you're a hard-ass and everything you cook is slop, but the strength you bring to the table makes up for that."

Coba spoke with no trace of spite, but Chrome just glared at him.

"Tact was never your forte."

"And good humor was never yours. This is the era of smiles, my old friend."

Coba flashed a phony grin. Chrome's lips formed the exact opposite.

"Please?" Coba asked. "If a guest is injured, it'll be a disaster. That's the last thing I need...and this is a major holiday. The hotel's booked, and I need every hand I can get. I don't want to screw this up and get docked a star in the hotel guide."

"I feel like they'd dock you a star the second you hired a hard-ass like me."

Chrome seemed to be holding that line against him, but Coba just laughed and clapped him on the shoulder.

"Even military academy staff are free for the holidays, right? And you said you quit running the meal hall. So who *is* running this place? A competitor?"

"Oh, well..."

That was when...

"————gh!!" Coba's back stiffened, his fists unconsciously clenching, ready for a fight. "What...is that?!" he wheezed, his voice almost drowned out by the beating of his heart.

Thud. Thud. Thud.

Sweat ran down his forehead. Steam rose from it.

He had the look of a man realizing he'd just stepped into a monster's den.

He turned slowly, to see...

"Here you are! Two cups of tea."

...a boy with a gentle smile carrying the order.

"Hi-yahhhhhhhh!"

As if an enemy had snuck up behind him, Coba spun around and delivered a backhanded swing.

It was kill or be killed.

The whoosh of his sudden motion echoed through the meal hall.

Lloyd leaned back just enough to avoid Coba's fist, moving so fast he left an afterimage—all without spilling a drop of tea.

Coba gasped, stunned.

"Wh-who *are* you?!" he croaked.

"Oh, my name's Lloyd Belladonna," the boy said, smiling. "I took over this meal hall from Chrome!"

He bowed politely and placed the tea on the table as if nothing had happened.

"Sorry. Am I interrupting your calisthenics?"

"Huh? Calisthenics?"

Coba might have been retired, but he was pretty confident the force of his blow was still every bit as impressive as that of any active cadet. Having it dismissed as "calisthenics" was simply baffling.

"Lloyd, how about we get two risotto started?"

"Oh, certainly! Coming right up, Chrome!" Lloyd bowed again and hustled back to the kitchen.

Coba was left staring after him.

"Sit down, Coba," Chrome urged, as if this happened a lot.

Coba silently settled into his chair, all expression draining from his face.

Chrome grinned at him. "What happened to the whole smile thing?" he asked, clearly relishing this.

Coba didn't seem to notice. He leaned over the table, his tone urgent. "Wh-who the hell is that...*monster*?!"

"Lloyd. A cadet at the military academy."

"B-bullshit! No way a beast like that is a student!"

"Pretty much my reaction," Chrome admitted. "But I swear, he *is* one of my students. Just, well...he's from—"

Chrome broke off, thinking better of it.

Lloyd was from a village named Kunlun: a legendary town where heroes gathered, known far and wide...in children's stories.

Saying Lloyd was actually from there would only make Coba laugh.

"Mm? From where?"

"Uh...way out in the boonies. He's doing his best to become a good soldier and send money back home. A real good kid."

That was 99 percent true! Yet somehow fundamentally wrong.

"A struggling student? I suppose people out in the boonies have to learn to fend off horrible monsters. Makes sense he'd get that strong."

This guess was more or less on target. Except Lloyd had grown up fending off far more horrible demon lords.

Chrome settled for an awkward smile, and Coba shook his head, impressed. Then Lloyd reemerged with their dishes.

"Here's your risotto!"

The steam carried the tang of tomatoes to their nostrils. The parsley garnish added an appetizing touch of green, perfectly balancing the dish's colors. Coba examined the food with wide eyes, clearly certain this would be an excellent meal.

He took a spoonful.

He chewed slowly, savoring the flawless harmony between the tart tomatoes and the sweet rice.

"Makes you feel like an accordion player."

"What's that even mean, Coba?!"

"I want to give it a standing ovation."

"Sit down, Coba!" Chrome shook his head at his former boss's ecstatic review.

When their plates were clean, Coba fixed Chrome with an earnest look.

"Chrome...can I borrow that kid?"

"Lloyd?"

Coba nodded. "He's strong. He's a fantastic cook. And his customer service is top-notch! Of course I want to hire him! I'll even splurge on the wages!"

"Yeah, but...it's not up to me."

Coba took a firm grip on Chrome's square shoulders. What a passionate portrait of two men!

"I'm begging you! Can we at least talk about it?!"

"Uh, Coba! That hurts! And people are beginning to stare."

"Please! I'll do anything! I'll hound you every day until you say yes!"

Chrome could sense the crowd around them shrinking away. He turned red. "Calm down!" he begged. But his red face was just making it worse.

In the end, he was forced to fold in the face of his ex-boss's excitement. Chrome ran the idea by Lloyd.

"Oh, I don't mind," Lloyd said. "I don't have any plans, and the meal hall will be closed for the holidays."

And thus, Chrome successfully avoided false rumors about his interest in men, even after everyone had seen this passionate exchange between him and his ex-boss.

—I mean, Lloyd agreed to work as holiday staff at a hotel.

An Inescapable Suspicion: Suppose You Found Someone Standing Over a Dead Body Holding a Weapon

Azami Military Academy. House of learning, where young hopefuls trained day and night.

On a break from training, Riho came over to Lloyd to chat. Riho had narrow, crafty eyes and a bulky mithril arm that totally didn't match her slim build; everything about her screamed villain.

When a girl like her sat down next to a gentle-looking kid like Lloyd, it pretty much looked like she was there to mug him.

"Yo, Lloyd, got a question for you."

"Oh, sure. What?" He put a bookmark in the novel he was in the middle of and looked up.

"Sorry, you were reading?"

"Oh, don't worry. I've read it so many times… This scene in particular is so good, I've basically memorized it."

Riho glanced at the book's cover and saw some sort of soldier wielding an ancient weapon in battle. It was a hardcover, but Lloyd had read it so many times, the corners were frayed.

"That about a soldier traveling the world and fighting evil armies?"

"This book inspired me to become a soldier. It's basically my bible. Possibly a childish bible…"

Riho was prone to making fun of comments like that, but Lloyd's open smile and earnest delivery did a number on her. Rubbing her flushed cheeks to hide her embarrassment, she decided to get to the point.

"So, uh, we've got this holiday coming up, right? Would you be free to join me on a thing?"

She seemed a little shy, but the invitation was awkward for Lloyd in a totally different way.

"Sorry, uh, I already have a job lined up."

"A job? Monster exterminating, or…?"

"No, no, if I tried to help exterminate monsters, I'd just get in everyone's way."

"Right…"

Riho bit her tongue. This boy's chronically low self-esteem wasn't really improving, and the contrast between his perception of himself and his actual abilities was dizzying, seeing as he could take out your average army and just about any monster.

But Riho let his comment pass. What else was there to be said at this point?

"So what's the job?"

"I haven't been told that much, but helping in the kitchen at some big inn."

No one would deny this kid had the makings of a great housewife. Riho had seen firsthand what he could do in a kitchen.

"Oh, that makes sense," she said, disappointed. "And here I figured I could teach you what grown-ups do for fun."

Suddenly, there was a chill in the air, and a blond girl appeared behind her.

"Why, hello, everyone," the girl growled.

Her name was Selen Hemein. Formerly known as the Cursed Belt Princess, she'd been something of an urban legend back home. But the belt cursed to never come off had been defeated by Lloyd's power, making her scary obsessed with him.

Whenever they got a day off, she'd show up to cheerily pressure Lloyd into a date…but not this time.

"What's up, m'lady? You're usually wide-eyed, begging Lloyd to go out with you… Trying a new approach?" Riho guessed.

"No…I've actually been summoned back home."

"And that's got you this depressed?"

Selen frantically mussed her own hair. "A real holiday! All my plans for a romantic trip to the hot springs with Sir Lloyd, totally destroyed! No consideration for the work I put into planning—for nothing!"

The belt at her hips was writhing around with this emotional outburst. The cursed belt was now an artifact she controlled at will, which meant there was no telling what it would do if she got upset.

"Did she run these plans by you, Lloyd?"

"No, first I've heard of them."

"M'lady...seems like you're the one with no consideration."

Selen had crumpled into a teary mess and wasn't listening. "Aah, what if they tell me I can't come back?!"

"Heh-heh-heh, then we'll finally have some peace and quiet around here."

"I've prepared for the worst! I ordered some bottle bombs to take with me so I can turn the place into a sea of fire at the first sign of trouble."

"That definitely sounds like your worst idea yet."

"Sorry. It's all because I took this job... I appreciate your invitation, but I doubt I can take you up on it."

Lloyd's kindness provoked an even more dramatic reaction from Selen. Apparently, his words were the only ones her ears could hear.

"You appreciate the invite? That means you'll definitely say yes next time! And that means we're as good as married!"

Selen's brain was already churning out more sweet dreams. While she was busy with her mental gymnastics, Riho shook her head.

"A leap too far, m'lady. Marriage isn't in the cards."

"No, Riho, your vibe has changed in a subtle but ominous way, so I need to arrange a shotgun wedding before that threat manifests."

Thanks to the events at the Student Sorcery Tournament, Riho had started looking at Lloyd in a different light. She denied it, but...

"H-hey! D-don't joke about..."

Red-faced. Spluttering. Her weak response was a dead giveaway.

"You *have* changed, Riho. It's like you're cuter now," Lloyd said, dealing the finishing blow without the slightest clue what effect it would have.

©Nao Watanuki

"L-Lloyd, you—!"

"This calls for drastic measures," Selen hissed, radiating hostility. But before she could act on it...

"Mm."

...someone suddenly put Lloyd in a headlock.

"Ph-Phyllo!"

It was Phyllo Quinone, a martial artist who'd enlisted quite recently. Never very talkative, she was a tall blonde with a model's build whose physical strength rivaled Lloyd's. She was prone to causing property damage at a moment's notice.

Without so much as the twitch of an eyebrow, she wrapped her arms around Lloyd, squeezing him tight against her chest.

"What are you doing?!"

"What's the big idea?!"

"I can't see my master during the holidays...so I'm getting my fill of him now."

"Your fill of *what*?! And how long have you been listening?"

"'Asking Lloyd out is nerve-racking, but I'd better do it before Selen asks him. Well, it's not a date, just...strengthening our bonds. Not in a datey way, but...'"

"That's what I said to myself right after class ended!" Riho yelped. How closely had Phyllo been following her?

Then she realized Selen was glaring at her balefully.

"Rihoooo...you were *totally* trying to pull one over on me! You wanted a date with Sir Lloyd?!"

"No! And he already turned me down, anyway. So it doesn't count!"

"I'm helping my sister with her job over the holiday, so I can't hang out... So sad."

A rare display of emotion from Phyllo, who sounded so dejected that all the girls hung their heads. Everyone was mad for Lloyd, huh?

Just as all the girls looked ready to head to a wake, a boisterous man barreled in behind them. Over six feet tall, Allan was the total warrior package and had appointed himself Lloyd's student.

"Tough luck, mercenary! But don't worry. The best path to a date is to ask repeatedly until you finally wear them down."

"Why are you acting like you know what you're talking about…? And I wasn't asking him on a date! Just trying to show him how adults have fun!"

"So you were attempting to instill your vices in him?! Sir Lloyd, don't you ever go anywhere with this lady. There's no telling what trouble it could lead to."

Riho shrugged Allan off. "Big talk, buddy. I was planning on taking him to the favorite pastime of the idle rich: a little equestrian sporting. Train his eye to the aesthetics of the thing."

She meant the racetrack, clearly. Allan just shook his head.

"Really, gambling? Good thing you took that job, Lloyd. I have plans myself, so I wouldn't have been around to protect you."

"What plans do you have, Allan?" Lloyd asked.

"Heh-heh." The big man grinned. "I know, as your student, I should be helping you with whatever work you've taken…but this was a duty I couldn't shirk. Sad but true."

His nostrils flared. He clearly wanted them to ask what duty he was referring to.

"Got it. Creepy. Please leave."

"That's just mean! Aren't you at all curious?!"

"Sure, that smirk is real curious. Curious how you have the nerve to show it in public."

"That's less curious than callous! You could at least feign interest in my affairs!"

"Um," Lloyd said dutifully. This was a student who demanded a lot from his master. "So what are you doing over the holidays?"

"Glad you asked, Lloyd!" Allan said, seizing his moment. He pulled himself up to his full height, expression confident. "You see, I'm meeting a potential bride."

"Creepy. Please leave," Riho said again.

"No interest in my affairs at all, huh?" Allan sulked, looking very sad. "Nope, nope, I can't let everything some tomboy says get under my skin. Not when I'm such a catch, I've got women personally asking for my hand."

This only made Riho's eyes narrow still further. "Pfft, you sure are letting this potential bride go to your head, Allan."

"Ha! Say what you like. Nobody makes these formal requests because they like your face—it's proof they've deemed you worthy of their hand."

"With that kind of worth, who needs money? Share some of your happiness with me," Riho said, swiping his wallet.

"Hey! Back up! That's not right!"

"What? You're a worthy man! You don't need a pretty face or a loaded wallet."

"That doesn't mean you can empty my wallet into yours!"

Both kinds of worth were important.

As Riho rifled through Allan's wallet, Selen and Phyllo peered over her shoulders.

"Oh, there's a four-leaf clover in here."

"Like a little girl."

"Knock that off!" Allan turned beet red. Despite his beefy exterior, he did have his feminine side.

"I think he's been a bit too cocky lately, so we should turn this into a three-leaf clover."

"God, don't! Do you have any idea how long I was crawling around the riverbank looking for that?!"

Ignoring his desperate grabs, Riho turned to Lloyd.

"So, Lloyd, tell me your favorite numbers. For future reference."

"You're gonna take my wallet to the racetrack?!"

"Um...four, three, and seven?"

"Going for the trifecta?"

"Lloyd! Don't answer her! Although it was really nice of you to do so!"

Allan's cries echoed through the room, but the other students barely glanced their way. Torturing Allan had become a routine part of their day.

At the time, the five of them had no way of knowing that their disparate plans for the holidays would bring them together in the most surprising fashion…

At her shop on the East Side—where Lloyd currently resided—Marie was enjoying a cup of tea.

Marie was a bespectacled fifteen-year-old wearing a pointy hat and a black dress with elaborate embellishments, both of which made her look very witchlike. She gave the impression of being somewhat older than her actual age; she'd lived through her share of hardship, conveying the illusion of maturity.

The East Side was like Detroit without RoboCop, or Gotham without Batman. In postapocalyptic terms, this was the kind of world where a dude with a Mohawk would go after a civilian, and the civilian would come back the next day with a posse to get revenge. Basically, it was a warmhearted community, in the sense that your heart never stopped racing enough to cool down. It would turn any girl into a tough cookie.

And that wasn't all. Marie's troubles kept piling up. Largely because—

"Marie! I came to play!"

"Pfft! Argh, Master! Stop bursting out of the closet without warning!"

—of this black-haired pigtailed pip-squeak, Alka, Marie's master and the chief of Kunlun, the village of superhumans. Her youthful appearance was frozen for all of time—in other words, she was your classic *loli* grandma.

Since Lloyd had begun living here, she'd started teleporting over, demanding food, sexually harassing the boy, or placing curses on Marie—a regular reign of tyranny. Sort of the exact opposite of a *zashiki-warashi*, or a childlike spirit quietly residing on family property.

"Gimme some tea, Marie. Extra sugar, loads of milk."

Marie reluctantly put the kettle back on.

"We talked about this!" she complained. "You're bad for the heart, so please call ahead!"

"Never mind that! The military school holidays start the day after tomorrow! He should be coming home… No, as the human representatives of the village, Lloyd and I should go to some hot springs and…"

Alka had spread out the official school schedule—something she absolutely should not have had—on the table and was drawing red circles on it, locking down Lloyd's time off.

"How did you even get that…?"

Alka just shot her a look. "I saw you being weirdly cheery the last few days and figured something was up, so I swiped it from the school."

"…………"

A cold sweat formed on Marie's brow.

"I figure you were assuming you'd be able to spend loads of time with Lloyd over the holidays and are planning something sad like inviting him shopping and pretending it's a date."

"………………"

Sweat was now dripping off Marie's chin.

"And you've been scouting locations you thought could generate the right mood! I heard you muttering, 'Lots of couples stroll through the park in the evening; it'll be perfect.'"

"Stop watching my every move! Don't you have anything better to do?!"

"I do! I've got mountains of work on my desk! During their busiest moments, people nevertheless find themselves spontaneously cleaning! Same thing!"

"You're stalking him with the mindset of a middle school student cramming for exams!" Said the girl who'd been scouting locations for imaginary dates. She'd turned bright red.

And with uncanny timing, Lloyd got home.

"Hello… Oh, Chief, you're he—"

"Welcome back, Lloyd! Ohhh, you've grown so big!" Alka dove headlong into his chest before he could even finish.

"Big? We just saw each other!"

"Nonsense! It only takes three days for a man to change beyond recognition! So I need to see all those changes close-up!"

Her carnal ambitions weren't even thinly disguised. Marie picked her up like a cat and dragged her away.

"Look at you... You're just a criminal now. First, you turn me into your server, and now you're forcing me to perform physical labor."

"Some server you are, serving an empty room all da— Augh!"

Marie dumped Alka unceremoniously on the floor. Perhaps that comment had cut a bit too close.

"A good server looks after the unwanted customers, too," she snapped, dusting off her hands. Then she settled into a chair, looking exhausted, wheezing like a retiree. She was *that* worn out.

Lloyd gave her a worried look. "You seem tired, Marie," he suggested. "Should I give you a massage?"

Faced with this unassuming concern, his gentle voice, his earnest expression, his pure expression of kindness...

"Really? Please!" Marie squeaked like an excited child.

"Eh-heh-heh...I'm glad it makes you happy. I'm almost as good at massages as I am at cooking and cleaning!"

He began rubbing Marie's shoulders immediately. Slow, then fast, then slow again, his fingers danced like a piano player's. Feeling like classical music was washing into her body through her shoulders, Marie closed her eyes, oblivious to the drool dribbling down her chin.

"Oh...that feels wonderful... I see... You really are good at this..."

"Yes," Lloyd said brightly. "This massage has been certified by Chief Alka herself!"

Marie's eyes snapped open in horror.

An instant later, his fingertips ran past her collarbone in the wrong direction...toward all the wrong places.

"Whoa, stop! Not there!" Marie leaped up before he could go any further.

"Huh? Wh-what's wrong?"

"I need a minute! That was getting a little too sexua— No, I mean, it was great! I just need more time! And like, prior consent!"

But Lloyd's expression was pure innocence. Just a healthy young boy! There wasn't a trace of ulterior motives.

And yet his fingers had... This was all too much for Marie.

Then Alka stopped wriggling around on the floor and shot to her feet, arms crossed.

©Nao Watanuki

"Yes, Lloyd, that massage can't be used willy-nilly! Not without my express permission—nay, not on anyone but me! That's the reason I taught it to you."

Marie's eyes glinted, and she grabbed a fistful of Alka's clothes, hoisting her into the air.

"*What* did you teach Lloyd?! This one really is a crime! A felony!"

Dangling in the air, Alka gave Marie an apologetic look.

"Listen, Marie." Her face broke into a grin. "Teaching stuff to innocent boys…is what this long life is for! Tee-hee!"

She had never looked more punchable.

"Don't brag about it! At least make excuses! Demonstrate some shred of regret!"

Marie was clearly in the right here, but Lloyd just looked confused.

"Um, so you really don't want a massage?"

Marie's morals were immediately shaken.

A devil and an angel began arguing internally.

ANGEL

"This is *not* how you want to get closer to him!"

DEVIL

"But it felt, like, totally amazing having his fingers sliding in, right? You totally gotta!"

ANGEL

"That's just using his innocence to move things along. It would never lead to a lasting relationship with Lloydie. A quiet deep freeze would settle in and never be thawed."

DEVIL

"But like, it was amaaaazing! It felt so good! Like, hawt."

ANGEL

"It certainly felt good, and it was real hawt, but…"

DEVIL

"No more *excuses*! You're too funny! Just go with what feels good, baby!"

ANGEL

"And in that instant, you'll be as bad as *her*!"

(ANGEL pointed at Alka.)
DEVIL
"...My bad."

Not the most articulate devil, huh?

But Marie certainly didn't want to be like Alka! This one thought allowed her to withstand Lloyd's temptation and redirect him to his next task.

"A-argh...Lloyd, shouldn't you get changed?"

"Oh, right. That reminds me...I picked up a holiday job, so I'll be out for the next three days."

All her holiday plans instantly crumbled. Marie's mind went blank. Her hand went limp, letting go of Alka's clothes.

"Oof!"

After the brief thrill of free fall, Alka landed face-first on the floor.

"Um, Lloyd...? What job?"

"Oh, Chrome asked me to help out a former boss of his."

"I'll have to kill him—I mean, how does that take the whole holiday?"

There was a stiffness to Marie's smile that Lloyd found unsettling.

"Uh...I heard it's a really big place and needs a lot of cleaning."

"Can't he do his own cleaning? Geez..."

Marie could have been talking about herself. Left to her own devices, she'd pile up dishes and pots like a puzzle game.

"Oh, also, because I'm a good cook, he wants me cooking for him."

"Can't he make his own food? How old is this guy?"

This time, it was Alka scowling... Marie might as well have been talking about her. Alive for over a century, yet she was still unable to cook anything edible. The same mindset that allowed her to use Excalibur as a carving knife made any other culinary outcome impossible.

But Lloyd hung in there gamely. "But if he needs help, I can't just ignore it... That's not the kind of soldier I want to be."

Lloyd had come to Azami to be a "good soldier" like the one in his favorite novel.

"Er...so I'm gonna head straight there after school tomorrow."

Knowing his motivations only too well, neither Alka nor Marie could argue further.

"Hmm…then I reckon I'll just have to show up while you're working and say hello."

"Just a short trip! Might be a nice change of pace."

They might not be able to stop him, but both were hell-bent on joining him.

They turned to get ready—oh, they already had clothes set aside and just needed a deck of cards. Cards were only useful once in a blue moon, which was what made it so tough to find them when they were needed most.

In the blink of an eye, two suitcases were ready to go, piled on the floor.

Both women grinned triumphantly.

Lloyd gave them an apologetic look. "Sorry," he said. "I know you're worried about me, but I'd really prefer you *not* come…"

This shocking pronouncement drained the color from both their faces.

"Er…Lloyd? You mean that?" Marie asked.

"Do you hate me now, Lloyd?!" Alka accused.

"That's not it. I just look at everyone around me and know I've got to do more on my own. And if you're both there, I know I'll just rely on you again. So…sorry."

On the outside, the pair *seemed* massively overprotective, when in reality they were just really hung up on him.

With his opinion expressed, Lloyd bowed his head and went to his room.

"Marie! Why didn't you argue with him?"

"How can I, when he's clearly thinking so hard about his future?"

Marie scratched her cheek, and Alka collapsed to the floor, despondent.

"How did it come to this?! And here I thought I'd finally get a chance to heal my weary bones by flirting with him all day and night in some deserted field!"

"I'm so glad I didn't try to convince him to let us go now…"

Alka turned on her. "You've got to think of a reason for us to tag along! Doesn't matter what! Do it, or I'll tell everyone you're the princess! You'll be driven out of the East Side!"

"That's unfair! Don't do that. Think of something yourself!"

That was right—Marie was technically the country's princess. There had been an attempted coup, and she'd been forced to hide here. Even now that peace had been restored, she continued running her shop, supporting the realm from the shadows.

Though that was mostly just so she had an excuse to keep living with Lloyd...

"Argh...all my plans, dashed!" Alka wailed.

"Grin and bear it. Even though Lloyd has so little confidence, he's finally trying to be independent. This is a good thing! I *thought* he was getting a little more manly..."

"He certainly seems more reliable than he did back home. Mwa-ha-ha."

A rapturous look spread across Alka's face, and a strand of drool landed on the floor. Mood swings were a characteristic trait of the kid-sized grandma.

Lloyd finished changing and emerged, ready to get dinner started.

"It's just yesterday's leftover curry, I'm afraid. Oh, and, Marie, I know I'll be gone a few days, but you can't just eat canned food the whole time. I'll make a few things tomorrow to tide you over."

"Oh, okay."

"And make sure you wash the dishes when you're done. Even if you don't have time, at least rinse them. If food dries on them, it's really hard to get off."

"Oh, okay."

"Then I'll get dinner ready, so can you wipe the table?"

With those motherly orders, Lloyd headed into the kitchen.

"Which of you needs to be more independent, again?"

"......"

Marie wiped the table down in silence, forced to admit she might be worse than Lloyd had ever been.

* * *

The Reiyoukaku Hotel was by a large lake at the midpoint of the merchant road connecting Rokujou, which lay on the western end of the continent, to Azami, in the east. It had once been a major lumber site, and the sides of the mountains were covered in cypress trees planted in eye-catching geometric patterns. A hidden gem for travelers, it had the same appeal as a hidden view of a city lit up at night.

As the lumber industry left, tourism increased. Shops and meal halls meant for lumberjacks began selling souvenirs and offering fine dining.

But the local inns were ill-suited to tourism, providing plain lodgings for workers and offering little for loaded tourists to drop money on.

Coba had spied an opening. Confident it would be a success, he'd built a luxury hotel, and his gamble was paying off in spades. They had a broad range of middle- and upper-class guests, and the hotel was even used for meetings of government officials or major merchants.

And with these important guests arriving for the big holiday, the string of victims turning up comatose could threaten the hotel's very survival.

"The coma thing is bad, but first and foremost, the hotel has to function properly..."

Standing at the hotel's entrance, Coba stared out at the cypress forests, reflecting on the past.

When the venture had first opened, he'd underestimated the challenges running it would pose, facing problem after problem. All kinds of troubles, everything from picky eaters to lousy drunks... But he'd overcome them all, finally making a success of it. It wouldn't do to start skimping now.

"Everyone's on edge, thanks to the incidents...but with that boy here, I think we might just pull it off."

Coba's thought were on Lloyd, the boy with the gentle smile. His skill in the kitchen was unimpeachable, but his physical prowess was even more impressive. And this superhuman had taken the job right away, no questions asked. Which actually suggested he might be worryingly naïve...

Coba folded his arms, watching the road in front of the hotel, his eyes turned toward Azami. It was evening, and the sun was already low in the sky, its glow reflecting off the skin of his head.

Yes…evening, the source of Coba's concern.

Is he really coming today?

Coba had told Lloyd it would be fine if couldn't make it till the following morning, but Lloyd had just said, "I'll head over after school wraps up for the day. Should be there by evening."

He'd made it sound simple.

Coba had laughed, assuming he was joking, but Chrome had replied, "Don't be surprised if he is." His tone had been so grim, Coba was left utterly confused.

He still found it hard to believe. And this left him with a suspicious glint in his eyes, like a cop carrying the ransom money, waiting for the kidnappers to arrive. The hotel sat on the crest of a hill, so he commanded a considerable view—and there was not a soul to be seen.

Still…that boy may be incredible, but I must have misheard him. Even on horseback, it's a half-day's ride.

There must have been some kind of mistake. Or it was a joke. Coba gave up and turned on his heel…

"Sorry I'm late!"

"Eek!"

Lloyd was standing right behind him. Coba let out an uncharacteristic shriek, his heart nearly leaping out of his chest.

"Uh…are you okay?" Lloyd frowned, looking concerned.

"Y-yeah…but why are you coming from *behind* the hotel?"

It was hard enough to sneak up on a former guard. But why he'd come from that direction was even more baffling.

"School wrapped up a little late," Lloyd explained. "So I took a shortcut through the forest."

"Uh…"

Was there a shortcut? Coba looked where Lloyd was pointing. He saw nothing but dense forest, tall mountains, steep cliffs…the most impassible landscape imaginable. That region was teeming with monsters, and Rokujou had declared it a danger zone. The road had been specifically built all the way over here to avoid the monsters in those mountains.

Lloyd looked a little embarrassed.

"Seemed like following the road would be a little roundabout, so I just made a beeline right here..."

Coba pictured the map of the terrain between Azami and the hotel. As the crow flies, a straight line *could* technically be drawn between the two points...but there were at least four mountains in the way.

Coba balled up that map and threw it away.

"I see! Well done. Welcome to my hotel! Welcome to Reiyoukaku!"

He decided not to think about it.

Lloyd bowed low. "Yes, sir! Lloyd Belladonna, reporting for duty!"

Lloyd's good manners helped Coba settle down. But...

I may have summoned a real monster here...

Coba saw more than a few monster hairs and cypress needles stuck to the boy's clothes.

Sensing a little awkwardness between them, Lloyd followed Coba as his new boss gave him a tour.

Surrounded by the bounty of nature and bathed in the light of the setting sun, the exterior of the elegant hotel promised an escape from the dreariness of everyday life. At the entrance was an area large enough to accommodate several carriages at once, yet not a speck of dirt anywhere. Rows of sweet-smelling flowers ensured that the odor of the horses didn't linger.

Inside, the lobby had been built to rival any theater, eliciting gasps from guests. As cramped as the big city was, Lloyd had rarely seen any interiors this open. The ceilings soared, giving it a luxurious feel, and there were plenty of seats around for guests to relax.

The entrance and front desk were manned by experienced-looking staff, greeting guests with smiles like they were welcoming family members back home.

The carpet was of a knot density so fine, trying to count them would be futile; there were paintings with artists' signatures more dazzling than the subjects themselves and vases that would clearly spell financial ruin if you shattered them. The sight would meet the approval of nobility who had spent a lifetime staring at such splendors.

"Wow! This is just… Wow! I've only read about places like this in books!"

The sheer grandeur of it all was making Lloyd act his age.

"Well, as the owner, I'm certainly glad to hear it."

"A-are you sure you want a country bumpkin working here?"

"Don't worry! Just follow my lead and listen to what your coworkers tell you. You've got the cooking and social skills already; it'll work out just fine. You okay starting work dressed like that?"

"Oh yeah! I'll listen carefully! I won't let you down!"

Coba couldn't help but smile. Then he led his new employee toward the baths.

Down a few corridors, Lloyd felt a chill in the air. A large, imposing bath spread before his eyes.

He first saw a magnificent fountain carved from a natural rock formation, filled with warm water to rinse your hands and feet. The ceiling was at least twice as high as that of your average room, with recessed skylights to let the steam escape.

Then came the main bath. It was so big, you could swim in it. The statue of a lion at the center made Lloyd feel like he'd stumbled across a ruin.

"This is incredible! I've never seen a bath like… Mm?"

At the lion's feet sat a woman with a mop, reading a magazine. She had medium-length, wavy reddish hair. The ends were in little curls that shone like she treated them with perfumed oils. Her eyes were downcast, but her lips and cheeks bore a touch of makeup, and her brows were clearly well maintained. Lloyd's first impression was that she took great care in her appearance.

She wore a cream-colored dress and a white apron, like a maid…but did not seem inclined to do any actual cleaning.

"…Hmm," she said. "Everyone's wearing white, are they?"

Oblivious to their arrival, she was completely absorbed in her reading. From what she'd said, Lloyd assumed it was a fashion magazine.

"Um…?" Lloyd said, looking to Coba for an explanation.

Coba slapped his bald head and strode rapidly toward her.

"Hey! Kikyou! No slacking!"

Coba's roar echoed through the bath. Kikyou hastily tucked her magazine inside her shirt and picked up the mop.

"Oh…ah-ha-ha… Fancy meeting you here, Owner!"

She only looked guilty for a fraction of a second before instantly pretending she'd been working the whole time.

"No reading magazines!"

"Magazines? What on earth are you talking about?"

"The one down your shirt!"

"I-I'm a growing girl!"

She thumped the bulge in her shirt. That was accompanied by a suspiciously magazine-like rustle.

"………"

"………"

There was more rustling as the magazine fell to the ground. Coba picked it up and crumpled it into a ball.

"Geez. I said to polish things! I take my eyes off you for one second…"

"But I *am* polished! Ah-ha-ha."

She pointed at the fashion magazine in his hand. He threw it on the floor.

"I didn't ask you to *look* more polished! I said polish the bath with your mop!"

Kikyou assumed a grave expression.

"But, Coba…"

"What?"

"Have you ever considered the feelings of a mop, being plunged headfirst into this filth?"

"Have you ever considered the feelings of an employer forced to hear that crap from his employees?"

The endless stream of excuses was finally wearing Coba down.

He turned listlessly to Lloyd and pointed a finger in Kikyou's direction.

"This is Kikyou. She's been around the block and knows her stuff if you can get her to focus for a minute..."

Kikyou seemed to notice Lloyd for the first time. She gave him a little wave and a smile. Not really the face of someone being scolded.

"Hi there! I'm Kikyou, currently recruiting cute boyfriends. Nice meeting you, kid."

"Uh...I'm Lloyd. I'm only here for the holidays, but I'm looking forward to working with you!"

Lloyd opted for a slightly more traditional greeting.

Kikyou folded her arms, nodding.

"Well, well, you've got your feet on the ground. I look forward to seeing what you become in like...five years?"

"I hope he doesn't learn the wrong lessons from you... Do your bit and show him the ropes. I'll be in the kitchen checking the pantry. Lloyd, if she starts slacking, kick her ass."

Coba stormed away, shaking his head.

"Man, the owner's got it tough. All that responsibility, and he's got to keep tabs on everyone under him... Best path in life is to avoid becoming important, live free, and take the roads most thrilling."

"Um..." Lloyd almost pointed out that she was the reason he had it tough but thought better of it.

Whether she was conscious of his unspoken opinion or not, Kikyou gave Lloyd a hearty smack on the shoulders.

"Don't be so stiff, kid! First-name basis here, okay?"

"Uh, sure."

She picked her magazine up off the floor, smoothing it out. "Have fun cleaning the bath!"

Kikyou wasted no time delegating her job to him.

"Uh...you want me to do all of it?"

Lloyd hadn't expected this and failed to hide his shock.

"Lloyd, in moments like this, you know what a real hotelman would say?" Kikyou struck a dramatic pose. "'Please, sit down! I'm totally capable of handling this easy job on my own!'"

She finished with an emphatic thumbs-up. Then she gestured for Lloyd to do the same.

"Come on!"

"Uh, right… I'm totally capable of handling this easy job on my own!"

"Yes! Brilliant! You have a future as a hotelman!"

"I—I do?"

"Yep, yep. A true hotelman would work himself to the bone for the guests. Particularly new staff! Every action you take must assist the guests or veteran staff!"

"G-good to know!"

"Mm-hmm. Have fun with the cleaniiing!"

"L-leave it to me!"

Kikyou sat back down and began reading her magazine again.

"…Wait…Lloyd, you can't just take me at my word here. You should definitely argue with…"

Feeling like she'd gone a bit too far, Kikyou looked back up…

"All done!" Lloyd announced happily.

"Ah-ha-ha, good one," she said, rattled. "Didn't take you for a prankster…uh…"

Her eyes narrowed as she looked around. The tiles gleamed like they'd been freshly installed.

With her mouth hanging open, Kikyou got up and ran a finger along the edge of the bath. It made a nice squeak. No residue.

"Uh, huh? How? What?" she spluttered.

"S-something wrong? I miss a spot?" Lloyd took this entirely the wrong way. "S-sorry!" he yelped. "I thought I got everything… Oh, the skylights! I'll go wipe those now."

"Er, no, not the—"

How had he scrubbed the entire place so fast? Before she could ask, her eyes bore witness to the unbelievable.

The mop gleamed magically, and Lloyd jumped all the way to the ceiling—two stories high—and caught the frame of the window.

"—skylight…?" she finished, her voice sinking into a whimper.

He wiped it once, and the entire room was enveloped in a blinding light. Even from this distance, she could tell it was now spotless.

"Hmm." Lloyd jumped back down like this was nothing and began polishing the baths again. "I'll give the bath another quick wipe-down to make sure I didn't miss anything else!"

He proceeded to wipe down not only the bath, but also every inch of the room housing it. Even the inside of the lion's mouth. This all happened very, very quickly. The bath sparkled without even a speck of mold, like it had just been built. Kikyou's eyes locked onto the glowing light surrounding his mop.

"...Uh, how are you doing this? What is that?"

"Um, a little household wisdom."

This household wisdom was actually a form of sigil magic involving ancient runes. Runes were a series of magical symbols that could be combined with magic to do just about anything, from disenchanting to teleporting to bringing down meteors.

What Lloyd had just used was a *disenchant* rune. Its side effect involved the removal of any dirt at all—which felt like sort of a waste. It was kind of like buying an expensive orange from a high-end fruit store and then using it to make a battery in a science experiment. Or buying a cut of tuna, deboning it, and then not even bothering to eat it.

"Okay, fine, but...how'd you move like that?"

"Huh? This is how I normally move."

Moving from one end of this giant bathroom to the other in a second flat, he'd traveled so fast, he'd become a blur. Kikyou had rubbed her eyes to the point that her eyeshadow was smeared.

"Like hell you did! You were zipping all over the place! That's no kinda normal!"

As she grappled with this impossibility, Coba appeared behind her.

"Lloyd, do you have a minute? Wow! This place is spotless!" Coba had to shield his eyes from the gleam.

"Oh, Owner! I just finished cleaning."

"It's been less than ten minutes... Well done, Lloyd! I see I was right to put my faith in you." Coba beamed.

Lloyd's smile was not as broad. "Oh, this is nothing. I just did the usual thing."

"No, no! Oh, sorry, there's something I could use a hand with. We've got room service uniforms in the staff room in back. Could you change into one of those?"

"Right away!"

Lloyd bowed his head and scrambled off.

Coba grinned after him. Kikyou, meanwhile, had no expression at all.

"Who *is* that kid?!" she snapped. "He cleaned the bath in seconds! He jumped all the way to the skylight! How is that possible?"

Her urgent tone was a far cry from her usual slacker drawl, and Coba looked momentarily guilty.

"That's a secret," he said impishly.

"...No! That's not fair! Also, please don't make that expression ever again."

"If you slack off, Lloyd will give you an earful! You finish up here and then go clean the stables. Do it right!"

With a sidelong glance at the stunned look on her face, Coba left the room.

"Um, are these the right clothes?"

Lloyd had finished changing and was waiting for Coba to catch up.

With a stiff collar, gold cuff links, and white gloves completing the ensemble, the uniform had a touch of military dress to it, befitting an upscale hotel.

"Oh, there you are! That looks pretty good! I'm sure you'll feel more comfortable in it soon."

Coba himself was in a black suit. The sheer bulk of the man's muscles was enough to make any suit look ill-fitting.

"Th-thanks. So what's this next job?"

Coba's expression clouded, and he slapped his head again.

"Right...you see, there's this important local lord coming. He was supposed to arrive tomorrow, but he's already here! Could you bring him something to eat?"

"Er…me? You're sure?"

"Yeah! You know how to deal with customers. Don't worry. Seems like this lord has a distaste for soldiers, myself included…but I'm the owner, so I just have to grin and bear it."

For a moment, Coba looked like a child being scolded.

"O-oh dear…"

"It's rough, Lloyd. He lives close by and stays here often… Rumor has it he's got his heart set on one of our staff or something. People have spotted them talking together any number of times."

"Well, that sounds romantic… In that case, he could stand to be a little nicer to you."

Coba nodded enthusiastically. "I've seen them talking myself, but…it seemed less like a love affair and more like a boss and an employee…but never mind that! You just act natural and keep smiling!"

Coba's own smile was incredibly forced.

Then he thumped his fists together and inhaled deeply. It seemed more like some sort of karate breathing exercise than anything else.

"…Whew. I wonder how he knew I used to be a soldier?"

Probably your every move, Lloyd thought, his smile somewhat strained.

In less than an hour, the kitchen had completed a number of dishes.

A Caesar salad with a generous heap of thick-cut, expensive cheese.

Roasted pheasant in red wine sauce.

Both would be served with a vintage bottle of wine from the cellars, so old you could see they'd had to wipe the dust off…and so forth.

Tantalizing scents and the sheer extravagance—Lloyd gulped for two different reasons altogether.

He placed the food on a two-tiered cart and followed Coba to the penthouse suite.

"Careful with it, and remember to smile."

"Yes, sir."

The silverware rattled as they approached. A middle-aged man with a broad forehead stepped forward from his post at the door—he looked like some sort of secretary. The bespectacled man was a bit too thin and had a perpetually exhausted expression. "What is it?" he asked.

"We've brought Lord Threonine's meal."

"This way," the secretary droned listlessly.

Inside the door was yet another hall, which led to the back. It opened onto a room with a massive glass window giving a breathtaking view of the lake. Standing before it, his back to them, was a very large man.

He had his hands clasped behind his back and was gazing at the view—yet his guard was up, and it was clear that if you approached him carelessly, your life would be cut short.

He seems less like a nobleman than a soldier, Lloyd thought.

The secretary called to him. "Sir, your meal is ready."

"Mm."

Even his grunt was dignified. He turned toward them. He had short but unruly hair, a strong nose, and rough-hewn features, and he walked like a commander on the battlefield.

"Lord Threonine, it's a pleasure to have you back with us," Coba said, bowing.

Threonine just snorted. He really did seem to dislike soldiers.

"We appreciate your prompt arrival. Did you finish work early?" Coba asked, gamely trying to make small talk.

"Something like that," Threonine grunted, shooting him a piercing glance. "You sound like you don't want me here."

"N-not at all, your lordship!"

Starting to sweat, Coba glanced at Lloyd, directing him to start serving the meal.

Lloyd obliged, looking only a little nervous. Threonine grabbed the bottle of wine and poured himself a glass.

"Sir, allow me to do that!" his secretary insisted, but Threonine silenced him with a look.

"We're not in a meeting here. Allow me to decide for myself how much I feel like drinking."

"Certainly, sir. I was just thinking the same thing!"

The secretary nodded vigorously, mussing his few remaining hairs.

Having filled his glass to the brim, Threonine rose to his feet, stared at the scenery, and drained the glass.

"The sight of these cypresses certainly makes the wine go down easy."

"They are magnificent, sir! Likely to be declared a cultural treasure! You clearly have an eye for quality."

The secretary leaped at his chance to praise his employer, who just looked annoyed.

"Silence. No need to respond when I'm talking to myself."

"Oh, right. Sorry."

Watching the secretary deflate, Coba felt a moment of pity. "Sir," he called to the man, "thank you for your kinds words. Those cypresses have helped make this a popular spot for sightseeing."

"Sightseeing..." Threonine sighed. Then he turned abruptly to Lloyd. "Boy, what do you make of them?"

"Ack!" Lloyd squeaked, snapping to attention.

"No need to stress. Just give me your honest impression."

Despite the luxuriousness of the penthouse, the intensity radiating off the man made his question feel like an interrogation. Coba was looking nervously from Lloyd to his guest.

"Well, I think they're pretty," Lloyd offered. A safe bet.

Coba shot him an approving look.

"Hmm..."

A trace of sadness passed over Threonine.

"But it does seem like a shame," Lloyd added. "To turn that into an attraction, I mean."

"Oh? Why, exactly? They're a cultural treasure! How is that a shame?" A smile appeared on Threonine's lips, and he moved closer to Lloyd.

"Well, it's difficult to get them spaced evenly and to grow straight. And they've even been pruned to eliminate knots. To do nothing more but look at them...it just seems like a waste."

"Oh? You know about pruning for knots?"

Threonine was getting steadily more enthusiastic, to the astonishment of his secretary and Coba.

"Yes, I'm from pretty deep in the boonies, so the village woodcutter taught me a thing or two."

Incidentally, in Lloyd's hometown of Kunlun, lumber generally came from a plant monster called a treant. Killing a monster that attacked with its roots and drained the life out of you wasn't easy.

"I see, I see! You know a lumberjack's pain, then! Before my family started getting all these medals, we made our fortune in lumber."

"I see."

"And my ancestors taught me the wonders of the lumber industry. It's in my bones! These hills may well be declared cultural treasures, but the beauty here is functional. If this is turned into a tourist attraction, its essence will be lost! I'm pleased to meet someone who shares my opinion at last."

He drained a second glassful of wine, let out a boozy sigh, and turned to the cypress forest again.

"And…if they're turned into a cultural treasure, I can't continue my investigation."

"Into what?" Coba asked. This had sounded significant.

But the wine was starting to take its toll, and Threonine didn't seem to hear him. He cast off his momentary despondency with a hearty laugh and took his seat.

"Bwa-ha-ha! Sorry, sorry! I'm bringing the room down! Aah, nobody understands the true beauty of that forest. No one understands the mountains and the trees. Everyone's just absorbed in how 'lovely' and 'beautiful' it is. Hearing that makes me cringe! But I like you, boy! Have a drink."

"Er, I'm on duty…and underage…"

"How modest! Like I was when I was your age! Bwa-ha-ha!"

It was obvious the two of them had nothing in common, but Lloyd just smiled his way through it.

"I've got a dumb son about your age… He's big enough, but that's about his only good quality. He seems to have got Azami fooled somehow, but… Oh, where are my manners? Have a seat!" Threonine turned to his secretary. "Hey! Get this boy a chair!" he snapped.

"Oh, e-excuse me! I was just about to! Here, boy. Please, have a seat."

Before he could protest, Lloyd found himself sitting down. He looked at Coba, searching for help.

"Go right ahead, Lloyd! Hotel staff serve at the whim of our guests," Coba said, smiling broadly. The perfect chance to improve Threonine's opinion of his hotel.

Working for a hotel must be hard...

Lloyd had no choice but to dine with the man.

Asked about his childhood, Lloyd told a few anecdotes about Kunlun. To him, they were totally ordinary events...but they, too, had a surprising effect on Threonine.

"My word! I never took you for such a comedian! That sounds more like a demon lord than a monster!"

"Uh...huh? A demon lord? But it was so weak!"

By the time he was finally released, Lloyd was thoroughly exhausted.

Coba and Lloyd left Threonine's room. Once they were back in the kitchen, they both sighed.

Coba slung his arm around Lloyd's shoulders. "Lloyd," he bellowed. "Thank you so much! You're the first person who ever got that man in a good mood."

"All I did was talk about home...and I ended up eating his food..."

He'd eaten, but he'd been far too nervous to taste a thing. This only made Lloyd feel even more guilty.

"That's totally fine! You earned it! Not everyone can sustain a conversation while dropping uproarious jokes about meeting dwarves or crossing mountains to shop!"

"Uh, those weren't jokes..."

Lloyd was confused by the way his true stories kept getting peals of laughter. But at this point, the other staff and cooks were gathering around them.

"Owner! You actually got that local lord in a good mood?"

"That really scowly one?"

"I thought he had it in for Azami in general!"

"Yes!" Coba nodded. "All thanks to the newbie, Lloyd! He got the man laughing so hard—and was even allowed to *dine* with him!"

The crowd let out an impressed "Ooh." Threonine must have left a very bad impression.

"Well, if he mellows out, that would be a huge relief."

"If he hates us so much, why does he come all the time? Spite?"

"You're the hotel's savior, boy! On my shoulders!"

"Erp?! Um, hey!"

"Not enough room here! Ha-ha-ha!"

Lloyd was getting increasingly flustered.

"But all I did was eat with him! I mean, I took his meal! Isn't there any more work I could do?"

"...Lloyd...you're such a good boy..."

His earnestness got everyone right in the heart!

Tears ran down Coba's chiseled features, and with a broad smile, he gave Lloyd his next assignments.

"All right, then! Clean the restaurant! Prep breakfast for tomorrow! Check and replace the light stones! Clean the lounge! There's a ton of work to do! You ready?"

"Yes, sir!"

"That's what I like to hear!"

Beaming, Coba began patting Lloyd's head with the sort of force that could cause a concussion.

"Ah! Hey, I'm not a chiiiiild!"

The rest of the staff roared with laughter.

This pleased Coba—he felt the mood had motivated everyone. But then he remembered something and looked around, frowning.

"...Where's Kikyou? She slacking off again? For Pete's sake."

I really might have to take action there, Coba thought...but he put it aside for now, focusing on rubbing Lloyd's head.

Meanwhile, a stray word from one of the staff reminded Lloyd of something.

Threonine said something about an investigation... I wonder what that's about?

Smoothing his ruffled hair, he concluded there was no point dwelling on it and turned his attention to his next task.

Late that night, in the Lena Suite, where Threonine was staying…

The lights were dimmed, allowing the moonlight to stream in through the windows.

"Are you retiring for the evening, sir?" asked the secretary.

"Mm," Threonine said, admiring the cypress forest again. "After that enjoyable meal, I've worn myself out and will be going to bed early."

"Very well, sir! I imagined you would be! Yes, yes, that boy was…"

"I just said I was tired."

"Er, yes, my apologies…" The secretary cringed, comb-over drooping. He bowed before taking his leave.

Threonine made sure he was gone, then turned his gaze back to the window. "…You can come out now," he called softly.

The curtains rustled, revealing a faint shadow.

"Good evening, Lord Threonine."

White blouse, reddish hair. It was Kikyou, bathed in moonlight.

With his eyes fixed firmly on the distant forest, Threonine spoke slowly. "Well? Have you found out what's behind these unconscious victims?"

"I'm afraid not."

"With all I'm paying you? The owner of this place visited the Azami Military Academy recently. Did that lead to anything?"

Kikyou winced at the mention of money. "Seems like he was just gathering additional staff for the holiday weekend."

"Hmm…I suppose he would know how to cover his tracks," Threonine spat, brow furrowed.

"This is just my gut feeling," Kikyou said, "but I don't think Coba Lamin is involved in these incidents."

"But he's a former soldier of Azami! They were the ones pushing for war with Jiou. With the princess missing and the king's condition unclear, there's no one keeping the military in check. We have to assume they're behind this mess, both to raise funds and to produce you-know-what."

Threonine certainly seemed sure, but Kikyou just scratched her cheek.

"I dunno...he just doesn't seem like the type," she said. In her mind, Coba was a harmless old codger, despite his battle-scarred exterior.

"Best to keep a clear mind," Threonine growled. "With all that's going on..."

Kikyou looked grave. "If someone really is breeding monsters near the hotel...and illegally cultivating treants..."

"Treants command a formidable price. One false move, though, and they'll disrupt the entire ecosystem, turning the place into a forest of death no man can venture near. I told you how fast they can spread, right?"

"Yes...when I accepted this job, you made it very clear how dangerous they are."

Treants were particularly dangerous for three main reasons: They were indistinguishable from ordinary trees, their roots could drain the life out of a man, and they propagated like crazy.

After draining enough energy, they could suddenly explode in number, turning an entire region into a natural dungeon. For this reason, treant seeds were illegal—not just dealing in them, but possessing them at all. Actively cultivating them was even worse. If treants were found growing anywhere, there would be immediate extermination quests posted at all guilds.

"A vast, fertile forest is the perfect spot to hide a treant plot. And a hotel run by a retired soldier from the Azami warmongers... On top of it all, people are showing up comatose in the vicinity, and their symptoms are suspiciously similar to those of treant victims!"

Threonine scowled at his reflection in the glass.

"Certainly good reasons to suspect the owner," Kikyou admitted.

"And oblivious to all this, people are turning this into a tourism hub... If they declare the forest a cultural treasure, it'll be even more difficult to search for the treants. We need proof before that happens..."

Threonine rubbed his temples, like this was all giving him a headache.

"But I don't think you need to investigate personally, your lordship. Couldn't you leave that to the border police?"

"This whole region is under my rule, so I can hardly leave it be. Several of my family's servants have fallen victim to it! That's why I've been forced to haul that suck-up of a secretary around with me… No, none of that's the real reason I'm here today."

Kikyou leaned forward, intrigued. "May I ask what is?"

"A lord I consider a personal nemesis has been doing rather well for himself…apparently buying up the treant wood and turning a profit on it."

"So he's the culprit?!" Kikyou yelped.

Threonine scowled. "Dealing the wood itself isn't illegal. When you defeat a treant, there are rare instances where quality wood is left behind…but the sheer volume they're handling is clearly something else. It's safe to assume these incidents must be connected to them."

"Oh…" Kikyou's eyes widened. "And you've got this meeting to discuss a potential marriage tomorrow! Is that why…?"

"Exactly. They chose this exact moment to propose a marriage to my son, Allan."

Allan's father, Threonine Toin Lidocaine, snorted derisively.

"I've got to turn this against them, squeeze information out of them, and prove Coba's complicity. I'd never entertain such an offer otherwise… Do you have any idea how much these fools have damaged the reputation of the local lords? The nouveaux riches, propped up by unscrupulous trades, and…"

"Um, I think I get your point."

Threonine was working himself up to an alarming degree. Kikyou regretting raising the matter at all.

"I hate to get my son mixed up in this…but the Lidocaine name was built by these mountains, and I will not have them sullied by treants."

Threonine gazed out at the cypress forest like it was his childhood home. An uncomfortable gloom settled over him, and Kikyou hastily attempted to change the subject.

"Any reason you got here earlier than anticipated?"

"Mm, I got my hands on some valuable intel… A while back, a treant sapling was stolen from a monster research laboratory."

"A sapling? Not a seed?"

"A treant sapling is already a monster…even worse than a seed. Once the sapling's fully grown, it'll scatter seeds, and then there's no containing the population. And…"

"And what?"

"This is a particularly vile species of treant. The laboratory were calling it the Demon Lord's Seedling."

That name made Kikyou's eyes go wide.

"The Demon Lord—in this day and age? You only hear that word in fables now. Like one day they just stopped appearing…"

They were still around! It was just that Kunlun villagers were dispatching them like any standard vermin.

"I dunno who stole it, but according to rumors, someone was peddling it in this very hotel."

"And then people started turning up comatose…"

Threonine sighed. He looked out at the moon, his eyes narrowing. "If they'd told people the moment it was stolen, this could have been nipped in the bud…but these fools were only looking to protect themselves. If we can secure the sapling, we can avoid disaster and prove that illegal cultivation of treants is happening…but we're running out of time."

"And from the number of victims, this monster has gathered a considerable amount of life energy already."

"Yes…and from what the lab says, this sapling doesn't need to move itself—it can be parasitic, latching onto a person or animal to broaden its range."

"So I've got an extra mission to locate whoever or whatever is under this thing's control? Does that get me a raise?"

Perhaps this was a sign she understood the gravity of the situation. That was the most generous interpretation of her inquiry.

Threonine gave her a half-smile. "...If you find this carrier, smear this ointment on them. The scent of it will force the treant out. Can you do that?"

"I'll certainly try."

She took a sniff of the large white medicine bottle, made a face, and put it her pocket.

"You can even mix it in their food. It'll slowly paralyze and eject the parasite. But rubbing it directly on them will have an immediate effect. Do whatever the situation requires."

"...Right, so how do I tell if they're infected? Searching blindly is a tall order."

Threonine scowled. "I asked around, but apparently, there is no visual change. To keep the host alive, though, their physical abilities increase dramatically."

"It does?"

"It's like a fibrous root spreading through the body like muscles, strengthening the host enough to compete against other monsters... Securing the target may be difficult."

Kikyou suddenly gasped.

"What?"

Lloyd's face had floated into her mind. She remembered his inhuman movements when cleaning the bath.

"That boy... It must be him?!"

"Mm? You know who it is?"

"Y-yeah. I met a boy today who jumped impossibly high! And..."

"Something else strange about him?"

She also remembered how impish Coba had looked. His expression took on new meaning. It had bugged her at the time, but now?

"When I asked Coba about the boy, he said it was a secret—in a really loaded way."

"I knew he was behind this! Damn the army of Azami..." Threonine's hands balled into fists.

"But the boy... If he is infected by a treant, he doesn't know it. He's a good kid, totally normal."

"Of course," Threonine said, dismissing her doubt. "That man is a vanguard of those craven curs in Azami. He infected a total stranger with this treant so he could deny involvement even if it was discovered...which suggests the rest of the staff are in the clear. Coba's behind it all..."

"So it *is* Coba," Kikyou muttered. "Guess I've got no eye for character..."

She gave Threonine a confident smile.

"Well, I'm on it. Now that we've got a target, there are any number of ways to handle it."

"Move carefully. Having this sapling as evidence will make an arrest far easier to arrange."

"Don't worry! I figured the need might arise, so I've been pretending to slack on the job. If I vanish unexpectedly, people will just think I'm at it again."

Threonine frowned.

"...Pretending?"

"Entirely an act."

"I seem to recall regularly asking for updates from you only for you to pretend you'd never received the request."

"To fool the enemy, first fool your allies. The best performances are all rooted in a little truth."

"Sounds like you just slacked off on work, then."

Kikyou responded with an innocent whistle.

Threonine clutched his head. "Well, worker of odd jobs...as long as you get results, I don't care how. You're the only one I can rely on..."

"Yeah, that yes-man secretary can't exactly handle this sort of thing... I can see why you hired me."

"He's capable enough when it comes to office work, but he's...physically weak and tries to butter me up at the slightest provocation...not to mention insisting his receding hairline is just a large forehead. Fatal flaws..."

He seems ready to gripe until the sun rises, Kikyou thought. She quickly cut him off and made a hasty exit.

* * *

People called her the odd-jobs girl.

Kikyou hailed from the famous Rokujou Sorcery Academy. When she'd attended, its graduates had still been considered the cream of the crop.

Even at school, she'd stood out—and not because her magic was strong. It was because of her sheer energy.

Asked to get a magic ingredient, she'd throw herself into the task.

Asked to help with a magic experiment, she'd help research the chant with you.

Asked to hang out, she'd be there, no questions asked.

Asked what she wanted to be in the future, she didn't just say mage—she'd say actress or writer or detective instead. She never held on to the same dream for more than a month at a time.

She did or wanted to do *everything*. In time, people started calling her the odd-jobs girl.

Since she could and would do just about anything, she happily accepted the name.

After graduating, she never took steady work—living up to her nickname, she made her living doing odd jobs.

If I've got a target, it's time to take action.

She slipped quickly through the sleep-shrouded hotel. Her steps made no sound, and she navigated by the light of the moon...until she saw the kitchen still lit up.

If the lights are on at this hour...

From a safe distance, she scanned the kitchen's interior and saw Lloyd standing there, sleeves rolled up.

Thought so. Doing prep... He's a real go-getter.

Restaurant prep meant getting all the ingredients ready: cutting vegetables to pile on salads, for example. Doing prep work in the evening saved time in the morning.

Figuring this was her chance, Kikyou readied herself to sneak up behind him...but the next thing she saw made her stop in her tracks.

...Hmm? That's a lot of veggies and fish...

There was a heap of food in front of him: cabbage, carrots, all kinds of veggies, fish, shrimp, an entire market's worth of seafood.

Before she could finish wondering what they were all for…

"And done," Lloyd said.

Gently, he swung the knife in his hand

…And in the blink of an eye…all the ingredients were sliced. Not just sliced and diced. The fish were filleted; the shrimp shelled; the carrots peeled; the potatoes peeled (with their eyes removed) and turned into bite-sized cubes.

…*What?*

Kikyou's jaw dropped. A wave of indescribable fear ran over her.

It was like she'd just found a crane weaving cloth with its wings. Sweat ran down her brow. She had a feeling she should never have seen this.

His carving knife was basically a multi-hit attack… How could she not be surprised? This was beyond shocking.

Lord Threonine said it raised physical skills, but…isn't this taking it too far? If I'd been standing anywhere near him, I'd be dead… Treants are truly terrifying.

If she'd known treants had nothing to do with this and it was just Lloyd's default state, her jaw would probably have dislocated.

Sneaking up on anyone who could do that with a knife was clearly suicide. Kikyou quickly changed tactics.

She grabbed a pot and a tea bag from the restaurant, plastered her best smile on her face, and called out, "Hard at work, huh? Prep?"

"Oh, Kikyou! Evening!"

Lloyd bowed his head low. Such good manners! Almost enough to make her forget about the whole multi-hit attack thing.

Kikyou relaxed a little.

He…really doesn't seem to know he's infected by a treant. Poor kid…

Because he wasn't!

Lloyd washed the veggie scraps off his hands, then saw the pot she was holding.

"You here to make tea?"

"Mm, uh…yeah, I-I'm on night patrol… There've been people falling into comas lately… I figured I was due for a break, could use a cup of tea."

The lie felt a little forced, but she was scrambling to cover. When she mentioned the incidents, Lloyd pounced.

"Th-that sounds awful! Comas?! This is a major problem!"

Kikyou put the pot on the fire, starting the water boiling. "Yeah," she explained. "We keep finding staff lying on the roads or in the halls. No signs of injuries—like the life's been drained out of them. At first, we thought it was just a monster, but…"

"If it's not just a monster, then…you mean…"

"Yeah, it's most likely human. Nobody's seen any signs of a monster anywhere."

Lloyd's temperature was rising as fast as the pot.

"Well…as a cadet of Azami, I can't let that stand."

This phrase caught Kikyou off guard.

"Huh? Wait, you're a soldier-in-training?"

He sure didn't look it. Lloyd seemed well aware and looked sheepish.

"Er, uh, technically… I get that reaction a lot."

"Oh, uh…sorry."

"But my dream's come true at last! I want to be a soldier like in my favorite novel, so I can't stand by while something this bad is happening."

The fervent look in his eyes left Kikyou scratching her cheek.

Is that why? Tricking this freshly enlisted boy, turning him into a treant nursery… What an awful thing to do.

That extra bit of information weirdly fit the puzzle, locking Coba in at the top of her suspect list. Kikyou was starting to see his friendly smile as the skill of an experienced con man.

If I tell him he's unconsciously draining the life out of people…he'll be really sad.

What he was doing was the exact opposite of what he'd dreamed. She wanted to free him from that. With that in mind, she started steeping the tea.

She also added the medicine to the pot, making sure he didn't notice.

"...Here, made one for you!" she said, smiling. "Drink up!"

"Mm? You made me tea? You're sure?"

"Yep! Chug away!"

"Th-thanks."

Lloyd raised the cup to his lips, but before he could take a sip...

"Kikyou! There you are!"

Coba appeared in the door.

"C-Coba!" Lloyd spluttered, putting the cup down.

Kikyou was equally surprised. Coba was beet red, striding quickly toward her.

"I wondered why the lights were on! ...Oh, Lloyd, it's late, and we're putting you to work properly tomorrow, so go get some rest. Thanks for finishing up."

"Oh, sure! G-good night!"

Lloyd bowed, put the ingredients in the magically chilled cabinet, and left the kitchen.

"He did such a great job with the prep... What a wonderful boy. Meanwhile, you've been wandering all over the place, and now you're making tea? Who do you think you are?"

Coba grabbed the teacup and took a gulp.

"Ah! Hey!"

"Hmph. No tea for you...*blegh*!"

The unspeakably awful flavor made him spit it out.

"Whasinnis?" he spluttered, almost unintelligibly. But since he was forty-five and bald, this wasn't at all cute.

Coba's actions had Kikyou swearing under her breath.

Dammit! He blocked me from freeing Lloyd!

She had leaped wildly to conclusions.

"...Ah, at least my tongue's moving again. Kikyou! What the hell were you doing to Lloyd? If he drank this, he'd pass—"

Realization seemed to dawn. His eyes widened and then narrowed, glaring at Kikyou. It was a much fiercer glare than any he'd given her when he caught her slacking.

He's on to me! No, more likely his suspicion turned to conviction. He knows I work for Threonine!

Leaping to further conclusions, Kikyou nimbly leaped backward, grinning.

"Sorry, Owner…I mean, Coba Lamin. Looks like the jig's up, huh?"

"K-Kikyou?! You can't mean—"

"Would never do to spell it out—so I'll leave it to your imagination."

And with that, she took a firm grip on the bottle with the salve in it and left the kitchen through the window.

Fortunately, Lloyd himself is unaware. I might still have a chance to smear this on him, and then your schemes are foiled, Coba Lamin! Kikyou thought as she raced through the night.

She needed to tell Threonine her findings, stat!

Coba watched her go. Left alone in the kitchen, he sighed, rubbing his eye.

"I never figured Kikyou was the one putting people in comas…"

Seemed like she'd left a bit too much to his imagination. Or rather, Coba had let his imagination run wild.

"Illegal treant cultivation, huh… With all his vitality, Lloyd's a prime target. And Threonine's been coming here regularly since the cases began…and knows a lot about the forest… I bet he's probably aware of the best places to grow treants. With the hotel here now, they'll never grow short on victims…"

Coba felt like Inspector Zenigata, moments after Lupin says, "See ya around, Pops." Kikyou had gotten away clean, having done whatever she wanted, and he was left furious at himself for not realizing in time.

"That's why Threonine mentioned investigating…and he must be opposed to the cultural treasure thing because that'll make his operation harder. He and Kikyou were spotted talking several times… I figured he was just scolding her…"

An idea struck him.

"I *thought* it was weird she was so obvious about slacking off! That was all camouflage for her crimes! If she was always slacking, no one would suspect her if she was missing during an incident!"

That was just who she was. But everything seemed suspicious now.

"Right! This all started when Threonine started coming here! And this prospective bride comes from a family whose fortunes are on the rise from selling treant wood! That settles it! He's the crook, and Kikyou's his minion!"

Having connected all the dots, Coba furiously flexed the buttons off his shirt.

"So much to do... Tomorrow, I'll get that bastard by the tail! Secretly, so as not to worry the other guests..."

Coba snorted, tightening his fists...and went back to his room.

Meanwhile, Lloyd was also pretty fired up.

"Lots of work to do for the hotel, but...people turning up in comas? No cadet I know would just stand by! Monsters are scary, but...even Kikyou was patrolling. I've got to do my part!"

He never suspected she thought he was the source of the problem.

With suspicions on top of misunderstandings on top of distrust, Lloyd's first day at the hotel drew to a close.

Instant Regret: Suppose You Hung Out at Work on Your Day Off and Got Roped into Working for Free

"Now the final straightaway! Coming up on the outside! Looks like a lock for four, three, seven! The first race of the day and already a huge upset!"

"—Seriously?"

The first day of the holiday weekend, and Riho was standing by the racetrack on the outskirts of Azami, clutching her ticket.

"—*Seriously*?!"

She looked the ticket over again.

"Four, three, seven... Yep, that's it. I hit the trifecta!"

The first race of the day, hardly a major event.

Riho had happened to remember the numbers Lloyd had given her and placed a bet just for the hell of it. The win had unexpectedly proven to be huge, paying out over a hundred times what it had cost.

"Argh, Lloyd's done it again! He's really got it! Well, I guess I'm the one who's actually got it! Thank you, horsies, I love you!"

She closed her eyes, kissed the ticket, and ran off to cash it in.

Her back pocket stuffed with bills, grinning ear to ear, she began pondering how best to spend this windfall.

"Blowing it all on more races would be dumb. Gotta think of something better. I already paid the orphanage dues for the month—maybe I should treat myself for a change."

Maintenance on her mechanical arm? Nah. A good meal? Just as her excitement reached a fever pitch, her eyes landed on an ad on the wall.

"Hmm…it would be nice to do something out of the ordinary… Oooh."

The colored poster featured a drawing of a woman relaxing. Riho stepped closer, reading the fine print. It seemed to be an ad for a hotel or resort.

"They've got a hot spring? And it's not that far from here. I could get there this afternoon. That settles it!"

Nothing like a hot spring to ease one's weary bones. What better use for her money? With that in mind, Riho jumped aboard a carriage and told the coachman her destination.

"'Sup. Take me to this Reiyoukaku Hotel!"

The horses started moving, and Riho leaned back in her seat, kicking her feet up.

"I've spent too much time around m'lady! It's making me all tense. About time I pampered myself."

Blissfully unaware that this treat would lead to tragedy, Riho began humming to herself.

"Can't wait to hit that hot spring…and have a nice, relaxing vacation."

……Poor girl.

Meanwhile, in a room at Reiyoukaku, a big man was fidgeting in his seat.

His mind was elsewhere. His gaze kept drifting away. He looked rattled, like a culprit who knows the detective's on to him. His name was…

"Allan! Sit still."

Yeah, *that* Allan. Even after his father, Threonine, scolded him, all he managed was a quick, tight nod.

After a long silence, he managed to croak, "D-Dad, I mean…this is a potential marriage…"

Pretty pathetic. What happened to all his confidence?

"Have some water, sir," the secretary said.

"Th-thanks. *Gulp, gulp… Cough! Hack!*"

Allan tried chugging it down like a sports drink at a hydration station in the middle of a marathon before coughing violently.

Frustrated by all of this, Threonine brushed down his mustache like a veteran soldier chastising a recruit.

"Some tension is understandable, but don't worry. This was their idea. Be confident."

"Easy to say…"

Allan had gotten used to having no luck with the ladies, which meant he was ill-equipped to deal with the unexpected concept of a girl actually being interested. In these situations, he entered a downward spiral, afraid he'd turn the girl off and lose his one chance of avoiding a lifetime alone.

Ultimately, his solution was…

"I'm gonna go take a bath."

A baffling choice.

"Mm? Well, we've still got time, but why?" Threonine demanded, asking the obvious question.

"Sitting here fretting is killing me. I'm better off working up a sweat in the sauna!"

Before Threonine could call him an idiot, Allan made a beeline for the suite's private bath.

"That's no reason to— Hey! Come back here, Allan!"

Watching his son flee the scene, Threonine sighed deeply.

"Geez. Whatever his reputation is in Azami, that boy's as pathetic as ever… I figured the army just picked a big guy who'd look good on a poster."

Allan's accomplishments had certainly been embellished a bit, but he had done his best to help people, and the results of those actions were real. Just to be clear.

Unaware of this, Threonine sighed again and gave the ceiling a baleful glare.

"I was right not to mention what's been happening here to him…but so much for military training in Azami. Once this mess is dealt with, I'd better arrange for him to come back home."

Then he muttered, “That idiot,” under his breath and settled back in his chair.

Allan taking the unprecedented step of entering a sauna right before meeting a potential bride…would significantly alter Lloyd’s fate.

When she reached the hotel, Riho yelled, “Keep the change!” at the driver and left the carriage. She’d paid the exact fare, however, so naturally there *was* no change.

Before her were beautiful mountains, the sunlight glittering off a man-made lake, and a row of souvenir shops down the hill clearly packed, even from this distance.

“Nice. Really feels like a getaway! Right. First, an inn…no, a hotel!”

As an ex-mercenary, Riho’s idea of lodgings was the bare minimum: a communal bathroom and a shared kitchen to make your own grub. She’d never stayed in a fancy hotel.

When she entered Reiyoukaku Hotel, its sheer elegance made her gape like a middle-aged tourist.

“Wowzers! This looks more like a theater… Will there be an opera later?”

She looked around the opulently carpeted lobby, astounded.

“I’d be fine sleeping on these couches…maybe even this floor.”

Riho reached down and touched the carpeting. “That’s expensive,” she muttered. She eyed the vases and paintings. “They’ll never notice if I take one of those home with me.”

Only in video games can the hero do whatever they want to people’s vases. Riho, of course, was not that hero, but a shifty-eyed bad girl with an intimidating mechanical arm. She was immediately attracting the wrong kind of attention.

When she noticed this, she quickly made her way to the front desk to book a room.

The clerk cast a horrified look at her arm but quickly covered with a professional smile.

“Welcome! At the moment, all our regular rooms are reserved. Oh…

we did just have a cancellation for one of our luxury suites. Would that be acceptable?"

"Hmm, maybe it would? I mean, I know I look like the sort you'd put in a regular room, but I'm definitely in the mood to splurge. Maybe I should... Do I have enough?"

Riho pretended to stretch, giving him a glance of the wad of bills in her pocket.

"...I beg your pardon," the clerk said, swiftly recovering once again and waving for a bellboy.

"This way," the bellboy instructed. "Do watch your step."

Letting out a series of impressed noises, Riho followed the bellboy to a very ornate door.

"This will be your room, Miss Riho."

"......"

"The suites in our hotel are named after the legendary heroes who once saved the world. The suite at the back is the Sou Suite, and the annex houses the Lena Suite—"

"......"

"And your room is named the Alka Suite, after the priestess of salvation."

"......"

"Miss Riho?"

"Er, uh, yeah! Show me to my room!"

This was all looking far fancier than she'd anticipated, and the bellboy's words had gone in one ear and out the other. She hastily grabbed the handle to enter.

Clink.

"Seems like it's locked."

"Miss Riho, that's merely decoration, not a doorknob."

Riho turned a bit red. She gave the ornament she'd grabbed a good rub to cover.

"Well, it's a nice one! Really brings the vibe together!"

After a brief attempt at sounding like she'd simply been appraising it, she went inside.

Sweating slightly from embarrassment and stress, Riho looked around the room.

"Mm? This isn't a room…or not just…one room…"

The entrance had a little basket of roses filling the air with their fragrance.

"One room for dining and one for sleeping? So this is the bedroom…"

She put her back to the room like an operative invading. If she'd been wearing camo, this would totally have been a stealth mission.

Having safely cleared the bedroom, she wiped the sweat from her brow and plopped down on a nearby couch, but it was so ridiculously soft, she let out a gentle yelp.

"…I thought I was sinking into it…"

She'd come here to recuperate, but so far, this place was fraying her last nerve.

"Man, you can't take the poverty out of a girl…," she chuckled.

The art on the walls and the canopy over the bed were actively unsettling, and she was beginning to regret choosing this place.

Then she spied something on the dressing table.

"What's that?"

A trapezoidal object with some sort of crossbar resting on top—arched, like a scale, but at each end were two round things with holes in them. The piece was connected to the wall by a cord of some kind, like a fuse.

Some sort of avant-garde sculpture? Riho stared at it for a long moment before remembering.

"Wait…is it a telephone?"

The mysterious device was indeed a phone. The design of it might have blended with the décor of the suite, but it was definitely a phone.

"Wow…I thought only top military brass had access to these."

The cutting edge of civilization, right before her eyes… Curiosity got the better of her.

"Can I use it? Am I allowed?"

Relying purely on rumors she'd heard about the operation of these telephones, she gingerly picked up the receiver.

"Um...then I use the dial? What else do you do?"

She looked the stand over, but there was nothing to spin or push.

"Hunh? There's nothing—"

"Hello, front desk."

Her search was interrupted by a muffled voice. Apparently, this was a direct line to the reception desk.

Finding herself abruptly in the middle of a conversation left Riho somewhat flustered.

"Uh, um..."

"How may I help you?"

"Er, well... That isn't..."

She couldn't very well say she'd just been curious about how phones work, like some mischievous child. She had to talk her way out of this.

"Hello? Did you mean to call, or...?"

"Y-yes, I meant to! I, uh...um...want to request a massage!"

"A massage?"

"Right, right! Um, if you don't offer that, that's cool! Really! So, uh...bye?"

"Oh, wai—"

Breathing heavily, Riho slammed the receiver back in its cradle, sweat streaming down her face.

"I-I'm so tired..."

Without even wiping the sweat, she collapsed on the bed.

"The lady in the suite wants a massage," the man on the other end of the phone said, at a loss.

"...Probably just the usual: never seen a phone before, accidentally called us, and couldn't just admit it. Happens all the time," Coba said, looking annoyed. His eyes never left his notebook.

"But, well...she's sort of dangerous looking. Narrow eyes, weird mechanical arm...not the type we want complaining."

"Partying on ill-gotten gains? Yeah, that type can be a problem. No, wait..."

Coba began thinking furiously.

"Owner?"

"She might be an inspector for the hotel guide."

The receptionist's eyes went wide. "Ah!" he yelped. "A sudden cancellation, and then a girl who looks like a mercenary? It does seem like the sort of trick they'd pull."

"A rough-looking customer flashing cash, making demands…definitely a good test for a hotel. But a massage…" Coba scratched his head with the fountain pen. "Hmm, what to do," he muttered to himself.

Then Lloyd came in, dressed in a hotel uniform.

"I finished up that job… What's wrong?"

"Oh, Lloyd? You see…" Coba brought him up to speed.

"I'll handle that," Lloyd said happily. "She just needs a massage, right?"

"Er…you can do that?"

Lloyd puffed himself up proudly. "I'm real good at them! The village chief always said so."

He was referring, of course, to Alka, the super-clingy kid grandma.

Coba and the other staff within earshot all pictured a venerable elder getting a shoulder rub.

People started murmuring among themselves.

"What a good boy."

"How sweet."

The incident with Threonine the day before had Lloyd's reputation skyrocketing.

"Sorry about this, Lloyd. You already did so much yesterday… The chef was thrilled with all the prep in the kitchen, and the baths were still shining even by the time the staff used them."

"Ah-ha-ha, happy to help! I'll just go take care of this."

And thus, Lloyd headed for the suite, blissfully unaware that a friend lay waiting for him…

Coba watched him go with a smile, but another staff member came running up.

"C-Coba!"

"What's wrong?"

"Th-the delivery today has something in it that I—I don't know how to handle."

"What? What is it?"

"Bottle bombs! Several cases of them!"

"Huh?" Coba gaped at him. "As in...booze with a rag stuck in the top?"

"If we store those here, it could lead to a fire..."

"We can't keep anything that could endanger our guests. But if we destroy them and receive a complaint... Who would even have those with them? Hmm..."

He slapped his head, then made up his mind.

"Right! Pile them in a wagon so we can return them at a moment's notice, and if you don't hear anything today, send 'em back."

The staff nodded and ran out.

"Geez, one problem after another... If Lloyd weren't here, we'd have been donezo."

Coba sighed, and the staff nearby nodded. Lloyd's reputation was so good, it had already reached its peak for the day.

Meanwhile, in Riho's suite...

Riho was still sprawled on her bed, her face buried in pillows. Every now and then, she'd remember her blunder with the doorknob and let out a little groan.

This was a new black mark in her life, for sure. She was really regretting the attempt to live above her station.

"I feel like I'd get way more relaxing done at a merchant inn..."

Then she remembered her mistake again and thrashed her legs wildly.

At last, her flailing wore her out, and she fell asleep like a little child.

"Hello? Hellooo?"

Sounded like a familiar voice outside her door.

"Um...pardon the intrusion... Wait, Riho?!"

Mm? What, did I fall asleep?

Unsure how long she'd been out, she turned, wondering who was rubbing her back.

"What? Are you here, Riho? Did you fall prey to these coma cases? Wake up!"

Oh…I must be dreaming. Lloyd's in my dream… I'm as bad as Selen.

Certain she was dreaming, Riho blearily patted Lloyd on the cheek.

"Um, Riho? Wha—hngg!"

"So soft…and your lips, too… Wait, I'm not dreaming?! What the—?"

Her fingers were still mashed into Lloyd's lips.

"Riho!"

"Oh, s-sorry!"

"Uh… Not as sorry as I am. Why are you here?"

They had both turned bright red and scrambled to fill each other in.

"Uh…so this is the hotel you're working at? And you thought I was in a coma like these other victims? Man, you sure have a knack for finding trouble."

"I'm so glad you're all right! Did a horse really bring you gold in its mouth? That's amazing luck!"

Lloyd had taken her unusual turn of phrase literally, but Riho ignored that. It was definitely amazing luck either way.

Now that they were both up to speed, Lloyd broached the subject.

"So, you ready?"

"Mm? For what?"

"Your massage."

To set the scene:

They were seated side by side on a bed in a luxury hotel suite.

One was in a hotel uniform, ready to serve his guest's every need.

An unusual situation. A suggestive silence.

The only sound was the clock ticking.

"…………………………Yes?"

"All right, got it! I aim to please! Leave this to me!"

"Wh-whoa…!"

Riho was so rattled, she couldn't speak, but Lloyd just smiled.

"Sorry, I don't have any oil. Go ahead and lie down!"

"Uh, okay…"

Wondering what the oil was even *for*, Riho did as she was told.

"Facedown."

"...Oh, right."

Riho hastily turned over. Embarrassed, she buried her face in the bed. For the second time that day.

"So you can do massages?" Riho asked. Lloyd seemed uncharacteristically confident.

"Yeah, almost as good as cooking and cleaning!"

"...You're that good?"

"Yep. Village chief–approved!"

Riho pictured the grandma grinning with her nose bleeding, only one thing on her mind.

An alarming image flashed through her mind's eye. Obviously, it was a lewd one.

"Wait! Just for reference, what does this massage involve?"

"Um..." Lloyd began running down the specific menu.

He'd finish any moment now...

"Nope! No way in hell! That will get you arrested!"

"For a massage? Uh, how so?"

"That's *not* a massage! What the hell is your chief teaching you?!"

Riho looked even more tired now. So much for restoring her spirits.

"Oh...so no massage?"

Lloyd was disappointed. But the specifics he'd described were too much! Riho felt a little sorry for him...and a wicked temptation struck her.

"......Then..."

But before she could tell him to go ahead...

Briiiiiiiing!

"Aughhhh! I'm sorry!"

The phone on the dresser interrupted them. Having never heard one ring before, Riho panicked and threw her arms around Lloyd.

Lloyd was surprised by her surprise.

"R-Riho, don't worry. It's just the phone."

"I-is it the police calling because I was gonna accept your massage? Am I gonna be taken in for questioning? And then held in custody?!"

"My massages are not crimes!" Lloyd protested.

Then he picked up the phone, not wanting to leave the caller waiting.

"Hello, Lloyd speak— What?"

His eyes went wide, and he let out a little squeak.

"S-so it *is* the cops?!"

"W-we might need to call them. I mean..." Lloyd gulped, trying to calm himself. "They found someone passed out in the penthouse bathtub."

The penthouse in the annex—the Lena Suite—had a small outdoor bath for families to enjoy. After receiving word, Lloyd and Riho hurried over there.

The private bath had a sauna attached, an older one, with a hearth on one side and heated stones within. To raise the temperature in the room, one needed to splash water on the stones to generate steam.

But there was far too much steam in the room; a vast quantity billowed out of the skylight as if it were the open lid of a bamboo steamer.

By the time Lloyd and Riho arrived, the rescue was in progress. Staff had the sauna open and were carrying a man out.

Bare legs appeared through the steam clouds, followed by an exposed crotch, a burly chest, and finally a face both recognized—their classmate, Allan Toin Lidocaine, his cheeks bright red.

"Hang in there, Son!" Threonine yelled, shaking him. Shaking the unconscious is not actually advisable. But this was just Allan, so it was probably fine.

Coba was standing by, stone-faced, glaring at Threonine and Allan.

"What is this? A warning? They know I'm on to them? Nobody's stupid enough to stay in a sauna until they pass out right before meeting a potential bride..."

Except this guy.

Having ruled out fainting, Coba felt his thoughts running in all the wrong directions.

"I've got the man behind these coma cases right in front of me… I'm not letting him get away," he muttered.

Then he raised his voice, giving his staff directions in a slightly theatrical tone.

"Oh, dear! Seems your son has passed out! What a shame! We'll take him to the first-aid room right away."

Coba hoisted Allan onto his back and tried to haul him away.

"H-hey! Don't—"

Brushing off Threonine's protests, Coba left the room. As he did, he shot Threonine a meaningful grin seemingly along the lines of, *We've got you now! You can't leave without your son!*

But of course Threonine had no intention of leaving, so he read the grin in an entirely different light.

"Damn, he got the drop on me…attacking my son as a warning and then easily taking him hostage… I can't imagine Allan would stay in the sauna so long that he fainted—not just before meeting a possible bride…"

But it *was* possible to imagine, Threonine realized. This was all his boy's fault.

Threonine was left pounding the floor of the bathroom, convinced he was screwed.

"I should never have left Allan alone… Kikyou warned me to be on my guard around Coba, but… No, the biggest problem is this marriage arrangement. He's concocted the perfect excuse to get this meeting canceled and let them off the hook."

These nobles were making a fortune off treant wood, and this would prevent them from leaking intel. Threonine was impressed despite himself.

"I can't let that happen…not when I finally have a lead!"

He put his chin in his hands, muttering to himself, trying to figure out a plan. This made it hard for any of the hotel staff to approach him.

Meanwhile, Riho and Lloyd were at a total loss. After all, they'd just seen someone they knew hauled out of a sauna unconscious, wearing only a towel. In particular, Riho was making a face like she'd picked up a rock and found a wriggly bug under it. Allan in the nude was just that gross.

"So this was where he was meeting this bride candidate? Poor thing, guess that's canceled now… Serves him right for making me see that nastiness. Let's go, Lloyd."

Riho turned to find Lloyd no longer at her side—he was standing in front of Threonine.

"Sir, can I help you with anything?"

"Argh, if we just had the seedling, I could call the cops in now, but… Mm? Oh! Lloyd! Sorry, I'm a little preoccupied…"

But even as Threonine's craggy brow creased, Lloyd gave him a full-throttle thumbs-up.

"Don't worry, sir! We are at your service! Anytime you're in trouble, we're here for you!"

He was certainly living up to Kikyou's teachings the night before. His somewhat theatrical pose got everyone's attention.

There was a moment of silence.

Lloyd looked so confident that Threonine decided to beg for his help. "L-Lloyd! I could use a brilliant idea here!"

Lloyd wasn't expecting to have to provide brilliance. Perhaps he'd gotten a bit carried away.

With all eyes on him, the best he could come up with was…

"Um, well…right! I'll take Allan's place to discuss his marriage!"

The ol' switcharoo. But Lloyd was only five foot three, while Allan was over six and a half feet, so…that would hardly work. Even the most generous rounding could not possibly make up the dimensional discrepancy. Riho was forced to step in.

"Uh…a switcharoo? Don't be ridiculous, Lloyd. If you put Allan's face on a poster, nine out of ten people would think he was a wanted bandit, and the remaining one would assume it was there to ward off evil. Meanwhile you're just, like, cute. Not gonna work!"

Riho's merciless evaluation of Allan's appearance was every bit as blunt as her assessment of the plan's potential, but the reaction from the crowd?

"Lloyd...you'd do that for the hotel?"

"Lloyd can pull off anything!"

"I was worried for a moment there, but now I know it'll be okay!"

The consensus was 100 percent positive.

"Wow, everyone here sure loves Lloyd...," Riho said, rattled. She looked at Threonine, assuming Allan's father would realize the folly of the scheme. But he was clearly giving it serious consideration.

"Hmm...that would never have occurred to me. I'm very impressed, Lloyd!"

"Why are you in?! Of course it would never have occurred to you; they look nothing alike!"

How exactly had Lloyd earned the blind faith of the entire staff in a single day? Even for Lloyd, this was like he'd drugged them all. Riho was left with her jaw hanging open in disbelief.

Completely ignoring her, Threonine pounded Lloyd on the shoulder—like he was the son he'd always wanted.

"Right, Lloyd! Let's get ready to meet this bride! Sorry for causing a scene, everyone!"

This seemed to remind Lloyd of something.

"Um...but someone will have to do my other work for me..."

"Oh, right... I'm sure losing Lloyd will be a major blow, and this meeting could drag on all day..." Threonine stroked his chin, considering. "My secretary... No, too weak. And not good with people..."

"I'm not? S-sorry..." The secretary looked hurt by the latter comment but seemed well aware of his physical limitations. He let his scrawny arms hang limp.

This got the hotel staff talking among themselves.

"We need someone with experience."

"Someone who can handle anything. A jack-of-all-trades, or a mercenary..."

"Someone who understands the situation."

"Anyone know a mercenary?"

A moment later, all eyes turned toward Riho.

"Huh?" Her jaw dropped even farther.

""""You!""""

"Huh?!"

Eyes wide, thoroughly flustered, Riho found Lloyd clutching her hand.

"Please, Riho! You're the only one we can ask!"

His expression was pleading.

The sweat on her brow wasn't from the sauna's heat. Lloyd was holding her hand *very* tightly.

"Uh, well...if it's *you* asking..."

And so she found herself donning a hotel uniform.

......Poor thing.

A few hours earlier, Selen was sitting in a carriage from Azami, en route to her destination.

Bored with the view outside the window, she'd nodded off...and before she knew it, the carriage had stopped outside the Reiyoukaku Hotel. It was an impressive building surrounded by pastoral mountains—which left her wondering one thing.

"Why a hotel and not home?"

She stared up at it until her neck started to hurt, and then a familiar face appeared from within: Selen's father.

He wore a simple, pressed suit, like any office drone—but his cuff links and other accessories were top-notch. Anyone with an eye for those things would instantly know he was doing very well for himself.

Back straight, he strode quickly in her direction, looking her over as if evaluating a commodity.

"Thanks for coming, Selen," he said in a level tone. "I see the rumors that the belt came off are true."

"...Nice to see you, too, Father."

The cursed belt had been why Selen was forced to leave home to attend the military academy, so she found her father's welcome inherently suspicious and was a raging storm inside.

"Why are we at this hotel?" she asked, keeping her emotions in check for now.

But her father had already diverted his attention from her and was looking down at something in his hand—perhaps a hotel brochure. He'd completed the necessary checks—that was all Selen would get from him. She found herself moving farther away.

"We haven't seen in each other in a while," her father responded. "I thought we should at least dine somewhere decent." Like he'd expected the question and prepared the answer ahead of time.

Selen was getting increasingly alarmed. She stood in silence for a moment, and once her heart was still, she looked up at the hotel again. The stately construction and tasteful decor were obvious even at this distance. It certainly seemed likely that meals would be equally lavish.

"Well, if that's the case...," she began.

Then one of the hotel staff spotted her and came over. "Welcome to the Reiyoukaku, Miss Selen. We've prepared a room."

"No need," her father said, not batting an eye. "She can change in the side room."

"Understood. I'll have a bellboy bring the outfit there."

Before she knew it, Selen found herself inside—but not in a hotel room. This was clearly a waiting room or an antechamber of some kind. There was a number of large mirrors, and a closet offered enough clothes to stock a boutique.

"This is going a bit beyond a strict dress code...," she muttered.

Who dressed up this fancy to eat out? Selen's concerns were only growing.

That was when the hairstylist appeared. She smoothly seated Selen, ran a comb through her hair, and applied scented oils.

"All done. You've got beautiful hair, so it doesn't take much work. Lovely!"

"Th-thanks."

Would anyone do *this* before a meal? Selen might not have been very worldly—she was dimly aware of this—but was this how they did things in hotels? Her reflection in the mirror looked nervous.

The stylist outfitted Selen in a blue dress and some earrings with a subtle sparkle before nodding approvingly. Then she packed up her things, smiled, and gave Selen a pat on the shoulder.

"Good luck with the whole marriage thing!"

"Huh?"

The stylist left. There was an awkward silence.

A few minutes later, her father came in…wearing a tuxedo.

"Selen, all ready?"

"Hey! Back up! Marriage?! Did she say *marriage*?!"

Her father was as calm as she was alarmed.

"Yes," he said. He kept talking but never looked at her, zeroing in on his tie in the mirror. "He's an up-and-coming military man. Been in the papers several times, so he's clearly being groomed as the next face of the army. His name—"

"I don't care who he is! I already have someone! I met him at the Azami Military Academy, and our future is set in stone!"

It really wasn't.

But Selen's fury fell on deaf ears. Her father gave her a single glance, as if consulting a notebook.

"The question is whether you will remain in the military yourself. The original purpose of enlisting was to enable you to remove the belt. With that accomplished, staying there is pointless."

Her father's gaze swiftly wandered to the room's decor. Selen fell silent as he spoke, never looking at her.

"If military work gets you scarred, no nobleman will ever take you. And there's no guarantee that belt won't suddenly get stuck to you again… Best to settle the matter quickly."

Selen felt like she'd seen this look in his eyes before—the same day he'd sent her and the belt away.

He hadn't changed a bit.

He had the eyes of a sleazy merchant trying to pass off defective merchandise.

Selen gritted her teeth.

I knew better but still hoped…he would be like he once was.

"You can just sit there if you like. If this falls through, it won't be our only chance. Consider it practice."

He took out his watch. "It's time," he announced, like a guard telling a prisoner their interview is over, and began heading toward the exit.

When Selen failed to move, he paused in the doorway, not even turning around.

"Come on," he urged, avoiding eye contact as much as possible.

Treating me like this… I can't really blame him.

She knew how they'd ended up this way. All that time spent holed up in her room, treated like a ghost story—the Cursed Belt Princess.

She remembered how desperate he'd once been to free her.

"…I'm not obeying the man you are now. I'm doing this to repay the man who once fought tooth and nail to help me."

"Fine," he said, like it really didn't matter to him.

Selen let out a long sigh. Resigned, she headed to the main room, her beautiful dress trailing after her.

If anything happened, she could always run for it. At her waist was the former cursed belt, now an artifact she could control with her mind, whether for attack or defense. She had it curled around her dress like a matching ribbon. But first, she had to meet this suitor.

Regardless of her true nature, in that blue dress, with those earrings, her hair done up, and a little lipstick, Selen was a stunner. Regardless of her true nature.

I wish Lloyd could see me like this…

Telling herself she was just here to eat dinner, she stepped into the main hall. By the door was a fancy placard, clearly written by an expert calligrapher. It read…

For the Families of Hemein and Lidocaine.

"*—I'm meeting a potential bride over the holiday. Mwa-ha-ha.*"

Selen pictured Allan boasting about it back in class.

"I'm done here. Good-bye."

Selen made a U-turn, dress flaring, and headed for the hotel doors.

Her father instantly barred her path. She was left frozen, like the space around her had been blocked, cutting off her only route to escape.

"Wait, Selen."

"F-Father…h-how did you move so fast?" she stammered, genuinely shocked by this display of physical ability.

"None of your concern," he replied, glancing downward, like this was just a job to him. "But why did you run?"

"There's a big problem here! A physiological impossibility!"

"All you have to do is sit."

Moments later, she was in her seat. Even a chair this nice felt uncomfortable now.

Reluctantly, she looked across the table, but the prospective partner had yet to arrive. Allan's father, Threonine, was sitting next to an empty chair, looking extremely nervous.

Argh, I have to get away from here… Me and Allan, discussing a marriage? That would ruin my entire life! And people might use this as a pretext to force me and Lloyd apart. Oh, I forgot I ordered all those bottle bombs! I could go get… No, that's not happening. And after I had them rushed here… What now?!

How had she convinced anyone to take that rush delivery?

Selen racked her brain, but all she could come up with was…

I'll just have to make sure Allan dies here. To demonstrate my pure love for Lloyd…

…exactly the kind of plan she shouldn't have entertained. How did this happen?

She noted the precise positions of her knife and fork, estimating the distance between herself and the door through which she assumed Allan would enter.

Approximately six yards… If I used the belt to swing myself from that chandelier, I can easily clear that in a single bound and jam this fork in his throat…

Her mind in the zone of a perfect assassin, Selen kept her gaze fixed on the door.

Soon she could hear someone rushing up outside.

"O-oh, looks like my son is finally here!" Threonine said stiffly.

Selen waited for her moment to pounce.

God will forgive me. This is all for Lloyd for Lloyd for Lloyd...

Offering up a self-serving prayer, she saw a figure appear...

"Sorry I'm late!"

Standing in the doorway was a gentle-looking boy in a nice suit—Lloyd, posing as Allan.

Selen shot to her feet and leaped onto the table. Her eyes turned to hearts, and she started slobbering.

"Thank you, God!"

"Er? Huh? Selen—augh!"

The fathers exchanged flummoxed glances. They had no clue what was happening.

"Hmm...well, he seems to have done the trick, I suppose? I can see why the staff were sure this would work," Threonine muttered.

But Selen's father could not conceal his shock. A moment before, his daughter had barely allowed herself to be seated, and now she was throwing herself into the man's arms. As a result, there was no trace of his earlier composure.

"...Look at her fly..."

It certainly confused him seeing this earnest-looking boy instead of the hunkier man from the photos, but he was much more concerned with his daughter's sudden propensity for uncanny movement.

"Em...your meal?" a waiter asked, unsure when to start serving.

It seemed like something entirely different was on the menu here.

"Who cares about food?! Leave the young people to it!"

That wasn't something the young people were supposed to say themselves.

Not wanting the son switcharoo discovered, Threonine steered the conversation onward with a tense smile.

"Well, let us discuss...things...," he started.

He put his hands on the table like a cop in an interrogation, fixed

Selen's father with a piercing gaze, and leaned toward him. He had to catch the tail of the treant cultivator, and this was his one shot.

Selen's father picked up on the intensity and adjusted his collar.

"Yes, I, too, have matters to discuss."

An ominous vibe resonated between them.

Meanwhile, Selen was behaving downright absurdly, and before Lloyd could come to terms with the situation, she'd dragged him into the side room.

Inside a hotel linen closet, surrounded by white sheets and the scent of fabric softener, the wild thing was panting loudly, Lloyd in her clutches. Selen's despair a moment earlier had been utterly forgotten.

"God has answered my prayers! I never thought they were arranging a meeting to discuss marriage between us!"

It hadn't been much of a meeting. Just a quick grapple and then a drag-this-way. More of a marriage abduction.

"But I'm not about to waste this gift from God! Time for dinner, Sir Lloyd!"

Lloyd was still totally at a loss as to what Selen was doing here, but he managed to extract himself from her clutches and ask, "Why are you here, Selen?"

To which her reply was obvious: "For love!"

...Apparently, she was in no state for a real conversation.

"Well, we're in a hotel! Let's do what people do in hotels!"

Selen was acting on pure desire without any thought for why Lloyd had turned up. She hastily removed the belt from her waist and started raising the hem of her dress.

An instant later, Riho's mithril arm grabbed a handful of Selen's face. Riho was wearing a white blouse, like a member of the cleaning staff.

"What the hell are you doing? This isn't that kind of hotel! This is a family establishment!"

Selen's skull creaked, but to her detriment, she'd removed her belt.

"Owww...wh-where'd you come from, Riho? What are you doing here?"

"The horses brought me, dammit!"

"What does that even mean? Why are you dressed like a maid?"

"That's what I want to know! Why am I being forced to work for this hotel?!"

Lloyd tried to step in. "Um, can we assess the situation? I'm so lost."

Explanations commenced. Please hold.

"I see… So Allan's fallen victim to these incidents? Poor Allan."

Said the girl who'd been ready to kill him a minute ago.

"I'd like to stop whatever's causing this," Lloyd said. "Both for Allan, and to prevent any more customers from falling victim."

"Then I've got an excellent idea."

"You do?"

Selen grinned. But there was no light in her eyes.

"Sir Lloyd and I are currently in middle of a matrimonial meeting. Let's extend that into a date and investigate the local tourist attractions, searching for the culprit."

"Your 'ideas' always seem to be ways to twist the situation to your benefit…"

Riho had hit the nail on the head, but Selen pretended not to notice.

"If an incident just happened, the culprit can't have gone far… We need to search the area. Riho, you pose as a member of the hotel staff and check the interior of the building. We'll handle the outside. That way, no stone's left unturned."

"You even found an excuse to get me out of your hair!" Riho's cry echoed through the linen closet.

But Lloyd clearly thought it was an excellent idea. "I think that could work—a couple can move around without attracting attention."

"Really?!"

At this point, Coba poked his head in the door to see what all the yelling was about.

"Now what?" he asked. "More trouble? Hmm? Lloyd…in a tuxedo? And the guests from the suite room? What's going on?"

The three of them made an odd group if you weren't aware that they were in the same class. Coba looked suitably puzzled.

"Oh, the thing is..." Lloyd began introducing them and explained the proxy proposal situation.

Once briefed, Coba slapped his bald head. "Good Lord!" he cried. "So the guest from the suite, the boy who collapsed, and the prospective marriage partner are *all* friends of yours?"

His surprise soon faded, though, and he frowned.

"Hmm...but...a stand-in for a meeting to discuss an engagement?"

Coba had assumed Threonine would skip town; he had no clue why the lord would be so desperate to attend the meeting that he'd bring in a ringer. Of course, this was in large part because Coba entirely misunderstood Threonine's motivations.

Riho took this as her opportunity to gripe.

"Makes no sense, right? Why have hotel staff pose as your son? Wait...I'm supposed to be staying here, so having me work for you makes even *less* sense."

"Let's just put that aside for now. Threonine...why on earth...?"

"And this guy's the one in charge."

Apparently, Riho's issues paled in comparison to the Threonine enigma. She still wasn't pleased about being forced to work here but clearly wasn't getting anywhere arguing the point.

"So Riho will pose as hotel staff, and we'll pose as a couple on a date, investigating... The culprit may still be close by! As a member of the staff, I won't stand for any more damage to the hotel's reputation, and as a soldier of Azami, this entire situation is completely unacceptable."

"Yes, we're going on a date... Wait, no, as a soldier myself, I must take action."

Selen seemed every bit as motivated as Lloyd, for entirely different reasons.

"Lloyd," the old veteran said, his eyes filling with tears. "The three of you are the future of our army. As former member of the royal guard, I am so proud to see you all taking a stand for what's right."

"Yeah, me and the ditzy stalker aren't really doing that...," Riho protested.

But Coba still wasn't listening.

"Hmm, as long as his intentions are shrouded in mystery, best to keep the ruse going. Lloyd, play your part well and be careful!"

"Intentions? Whose intentions? The intentions of a hotel owner forcing his guests to work for him while the actual employee gets to go on a *date*?!"

Coba breezed right past Riho's final desperate cry, while Selen fixed her with a smug grin.

"Oh, it's almost like you're opposed to this date and budding engagement, Riho! What—are you jealous?"

Riho's reaction could not have been more transparent.

"D-don't be ridiculous! I'm not…not jealous. I'm…"

Coba was busy nodding to himself, oblivious to their conversation.

"I have utter faith in Lloyd! Whatever actions he takes will be integral to solving this whole thing. You have my permission to act as you see fit! Go, enjoy your date! And report everything that happens after!"

"You heard the man. The hotel owner has made a wise decision," said Selen.

"Hngg…"

If the owner approved, his new employee Riho could hardly argue, whether she'd meant to work here or not.

"So sorry, but…Riho, was it? There's something I could use your help with. Can you come to the stables?"

"The stables?"

"Yes, for…reasons, the person in charge isn't available…so no one's swept the place out."

The only thing you sweep out of a stable is horse poop. Riho looked suitably horrified. Selen clapped her hands over her mouth, grinning victoriously.

"*Snerk!* The horses led you here…and now you've got to investigate them! Make sure you're thorough."

"You make sure you're 'investigating,' too! Got it? You're *investigating*!"

Hammering that point home one last time, Riho stalked off toward the stables.

......Poor, poor thing.

The hotel stables. A number of delivery wagons were lined up, and the horses had their noses deep in feed bags. The stables had been clean when she'd seen them earlier, but now there were droppings scattered everywhere.

"The stable hand's not around...so the place needs a proper going-over."

"...Yeah, I can see that."

"Not a fan of horses?"

"I loved them this morning."

Coba didn't get what she meant but thanked her and went back inside.

Riho sighed and picked up a broom. As she cleaned, she tried to wrap her head around her current predicament.

"I won at the races, came to stay in a luxury hotel suite, and now I'm sweeping horse manure. How?! Argh!"

After venting her rage on the trash containers, a lump of dung ricocheted back toward her, and she barely managed to dodge it.

This killed what little enthusiasm she had left. She hung her head.

"This is karma... I should never have considered letting Lloyd massage me. That was so not me..."

Regretting her moment of temptation, Riho threw herself into cleaning, as if it was the punishment she deserved. She'd done a lot of things in her time as a mercenary, and looking after horses was naturally one of those. She applied herself to the task in front of her.

Once the manure was gone, she changed the horses' feed bags and gave them all fresh water. They had initially been a little wary of her mithril arm, but seeing her work seemed to calm them down.

"You're all relaxed now, huh? Lots of clever ones here. And such beautiful forms... If you were racehorses, I'd definitely bet on you."

She was talking to the fawn-colored horse she was grooming. It seemed to be enjoying the experience and closed its eyes.

"Don't go to sleep on me here... Oops, no, don't do that, ha-ha-ha!"

The horse had turned its head, rubbing its cheek against her. Then its ears twitched, and it looked the other way.

"Mm? What?" Riho followed its gaze and heard voices.

"Yes, that guest is *always*..."

"Ew, how awful."

Looked like a couple of the hotel cleaning staff griping around back. A familiar sight.

Same thing happens at any job... Girls can be scary.

But she was a girl, too! The pitch of their complaints was only getting worse.

"And that new girl, Kikyou, is always slacking."

"Right, the redhead? Always snooping around. Very suspicious."

Is it her fault I'm looking after the horses? I'll remember that.

Girls could be so scary!

Filing away yet another grudge, Riho kept an ear on the maids' conversation.

"Did you hear why that man canceled his suite reservation?"

"No, why?"

"Apparently, he just didn't like the suite's name."

"What? That's the most ridiculous thing I've ever heard."

Oh, so that's why they had a suite open on a holiday weekend.

Riho remembered the bellboy telling her the suite's name, but she'd been too out of it to listen.

"But that's suspicious, right? Demanding we change his room like that?"

"He looked like some sort of merchant, I think. Maybe a deliveryman?"

"They ended up moving him to 102. He's definitely not here for the sights. Why *is* he here?"

Room 102, huh? Got it.

They weren't done yet, though.

"I don't know if they're tourists or not, but the pair in 201 are weird, too. They've done nothing but order room service."

"And when I brought it up, there were a ton of empty plates stacked in their room. Are they feeding something?"

"Please."

Room 201, too...

Thoroughly satisfied with this round of gossip, the maids went back inside.

Riho watched them go, then muttered to herself, brushing the horse.

"Two promising leads, at least. A guest with a trumped-up reason for canceling his suite reservation, and a pair that might be feeding something they're not supposed to have."

The horse whinnied like it agreed with her.

"Right, better get this job wrapped up, find the culprit, and force Selen to end her *delightful* date, pronto."

That stalker had a screw loose. Left her to her own devices, there was no telling where she'd wind up dragging Lloyd. Riho turned her attention to cleaning the rest of the stables as quickly as possible.

A Bout of Wishful Thinking: Suppose You Pretended to Be Lovers...and That Totally Sparked Real Feelings!

Now on to Lloyd and Selen, at the scene of their fake date. They were strolling through a park, gazing at the artificial lake and the cypress forest. Selen was happily plastering herself against Lloyd, her eyes permanently locked on his face. She could at least have *tried* to enjoy the natural splendor around them.

"Eh-heh-heh."

Clearly, she'd elected to enjoy Lloyd's natural splendor instead.

In his tuxedo, he looked like a kid decked out for a special occasion, as did Selen in her blue dress. They were strolling arm in arm along the shore of the lake.

"Selen…this is a bit much."

"Sir Lloyd, this is how couples behave on dates."

She pulled his arm even tighter, and he looked ready to panic.

"Isn't the lake lovely, Sir Lloyd?" Selen asked. She hadn't even glanced its direction, so she must have viewed it in her mind's eye.

"Uh, yes," he said awkwardly.

Selen shook her head. "The proper response on a date is 'Not as lovely as you.'"

"Th-that's so embarrassing!"

"This is a performance, Sir Lloyd. If you don't put your heart into it, we won't look natural."

"N-not as lubbly as you…," Lloyd flubbed, doing his very best but not quite getting the words out.

"Mm! Once more! Encore!"

Oblivious to his consternation, Selen begged him to repeat the line. They did not look natural.

"N-not as lovely as you..."

"Perfect! Let's get married."

Selen's engines were running wild now. She produced a Popsicle and insisted they share it, going for the old indirect kiss. It certainly felt like *some* kind of performance.

Baffled by Selen's one-sided delight, Lloyd decided his best tactic was to change the subject.

"I certainly was surprised to see you back there, Selen."

"Me too! I narrowly avoided getting my hands dirty."

"Dirty how?"

"Oh, never mind that. Heh-heh-heh."

The following day's headline had very nearly read *Murder at the Reiyoukaku Hotel!* But Lloyd was better off not knowing that.

Looking puzzled, he inquired about her relationship with the businessman with whom she'd arrived.

"So was that man with you your father?"

Selen scowled. "Yes, unfortunately."

"That bad?"

This prompted Selen to launch into a lengthy diatribe about her problems at home. How her father's antiques collection had led to her getting cursed by the belt, how that had consigned her to her room, and how the moment he'd heard she was free of the belt, he had immediately begun attempting to arrange a marriage. She was frothing at the mouth by the end.

"...Can you believe it? 'The curse is lifted, go get married'! And he tried to set me up with *Allan*!"

"He's just worried about you," Lloyd offered soothingly.

"No," Selen said, frowning. "Not anymore. Once, maybe..."

Lloyd sensed she couldn't quite bring herself to hate the man.

"But he's still your father, right?" he reminded her, smiling gently. "I don't have one, so I think you're lucky."

Remembering that Lloyd was an orphan, Selen spluttered, "S-sorry...I totally forgot."

"Oh, no, don't worry about it. I was raised by the whole village, so the chief, and Grandpa Pyrid, and the woodcutter...even Shouma was like a brother to me... Mm?"

He suddenly broke off, feeling a strange sensation on his backside.

"What's wrong, Sir Lloyd?"

"I dunno. Maybe a bug bit me? It kind of stings."

Lloyd pointed at his butt, and Selen took a good look at his tight buns—only then did she notice and scoop up something pointy off the ground.

"Huh? What's this?"

"Something wrong, Selen?"

"Oh, don't worry about it, Sir Lloyd."

She took a close look at the object—the tip of a blow dart. She sniffed it, checking.

As Lloyd blinked at her, she started muttering.

"A neurosoporific? Fools. That would never work on Lloyd. I've been down that road... The culprit must be an amateur Lloydist. And I'm catching a whiff of lipstick... I sense a new man thief! I'll let her be for now..."

With some alarming statements in there, her deductions were complete. Selen glanced up to find Lloyd looking concerned.

"Um? Selen?"

"Don't worry. Oh—I need to make a quick stop in the bathroom. You wait in the footbath there!"

With that, Selen left his side.

Abruptly abandoned, Lloyd still looked confused but did as he was told.

"Argh, seriously?...Tranquilizer darts don't work?"

It was the odd-jobs girl, Kikyou—whom Selen had just described as an amateur Lloydist. Her plan this time had been to tranquilize him and then slap the anti-treant balm on him.

But the results? He didn't even notice.

"That soporific can put a wild animal down in ten seconds! Does the treant give him resistance? Threonine didn't mention anything about *that*..."

But facts were facts, and Kikyou had to accept them. Of course, Lloyd wasn't infected by any kind of treant and was just naturally resistant to all kinds of poison.

Having accepted her version of reality, Kikyou began scratching her head with the bottle in her hand. The balm inside would banish a treant infection. The bottle was full of it, and the scent it gave off was rather sharp, somewhere between herbs and jam.

"Okay, Kikyou, time to review the task at hand."

She fixed the doting couple with another glare—looking very much like a jealous stalker.

"Lloyd's infected by a treant, and the only way to save him is to rub this balm on him somehow."

She clutched her head again.

"Easily said! But the sapling has given him superpowers! And he's not even aware of them!"

She had no reason to put herself at risk to save him.

Nevertheless, Kikyou couldn't get his gentle smile out of her mind.

"...I can't just abandon the kid, huh. He doesn't deserve any of this."

She waited a few minutes, and Lloyd went into the footbath. Selen must have gone to fetch drinks or something.

"This may be my chance."

If he was relaxing in the footbath, he might let his guard down. She could sneak up from behind and smear the balm on him.

Kikyou quickly approached.

Breathing quietly, she moved stealthily through the crowd.

And just as she was about to take the lid off the bottle...

"Oh, I thought that was you, Kikyou!" Lloyd said, turning around. He was still several yards away.

"........gh!!"

She let out a silent shriek. She was very good at remaining unobtrusive and hadn't expected him to spot her.

"What's up?"

"Uh, um. I'm just on break. I saw you, figured I'd give you a bit of a start… Kinda backfired."

"Oh, really? Sorry, just felt your presence and turned around."

"Huh. My presence. Wow."

Lloyd's Zatoichi-level spatial awareness left Kikyou twitching. He might as well have been the blind blademaster himself.

Treants make their hosts this powerful? You've gotta tell me these things, Boss!

While she cursed Threonine under her breath, Lloyd looked at the bottle in her hands.

"What's that, Kikyou?"

"Uh…this is, um…well…"

Caught red-handed, she scrambled for an excuse.

"Uh, well, you seem like you've been working hard, so I was gonna offer you a massage."

Even she thought that was unconvincing and immediately winced, mad at herself.

Certain he'd cringe at the idea, she reluctantly took in his expression. But he was nodding earnestly.

"A massage? I was just thinking I should probably learn more about what a proper massage entails. This could be very educational!"

What an unexpectedly favorable response.

"Er, what?" she asked, momentarily dumbfounded.

"Apparently, the massages I know how to give are illegal. So please, it would be a huge help if you could show me what a proper massage is like."

"Oh, okay…"

Kikyou decided not to think about how a massage could be illegal. Lloyd certainly seemed to be extremely into this. The passion radiating off him was so intense, even the steam of the footbath seemed like an extension of his fervor.

Before she knew it, he was on his knees, bowing his head.

Kikyou scratched her head with the bottle. This was all going much too well, but sometimes things just worked out that way.

"Uh, okay, leave it to me."

She had no reason not to follow through, so time for a public massage lesson.

"Um...should I lie facedown?"

"Er, no, you can stay sitting up."

"Really? So real massages are fundamentally different!"

"Uh, then...if you can take your clothes off..."

"Mm, that much is the same."

Without hesitating at all, Lloyd stripped down to his underwear, taking his lesson so seriously, he completely forgot the crowd around them.

Kikyou could hear people snickering. Taking your clothes off in a footbath would certainly get you laughed at.

Geez, I dunno who taught him, but that is clearly not *a massage... Must've been a real villain.*

Feeling somewhat sorry for him, Kikyou decided to free him quickly and opened the lid of her bottle.

"What's that?"

"......Massage oil."

Oiling up a nearly naked boy in broad daylight was certainly daunting, but she had no choice.

His intense stare was also rattling her.

"Mind closing your eyes?" she requested, doing her best to smile.

He did as he was told. The little hag would have found this adorable.

Get this done before it starts going to your head...

Guilt wasn't the only thing welling up inside her. She quickly squeezed some balm on her hands and started rubbing it on his sides. The noises he made certainly made her cheeks burn, but per Threonine's instructions, she searched for the sapling.

She couldn't find any signs of it. She searched his back, under his arms, and his calves thoroughly, but found nothing but extremely smooth, beautiful skin. Naturally—he wasn't actually infected.

Uh…nothing? Wait, then…

There was only one area she hadn't touched yet. The only part still covered.

I can't…but…it's the only possibility remaining…

The sapling could be hiding inside. She was about to reach inside his underwear…when she sensed death approaching from behind.

"…!"

Fury. Resentment. A bundle of negative emotion that made her fingertips freeze.

Uh-oh…

Kikyou leaped away, sending up a spray of footbath water. A belt the color of blood snapped at the spot where she'd been standing.

A stir ran through the crowd. Radiating a pitch-black aura, Selen advanced toward Kikyou, every step emanating hatred. Her trademark belt—the cursed artifact that had tormented her for so long—had been curled around her waist like a ribbon but now responded to her fury, writhing wildly. Like bonito flakes sprinkled on *okonomiyaki*, a savory Japanese pancake.

Maybe that metaphor is a bit too cute, given the horrific look on Selen's face—she was moments away from crying tears of blood.

"Death!" she growled.

While Selen herself moved slowly, the belt snapped sideways with no warning.

Kikyou was forced to backflip out of range.

"What the…?"

"I know tourist traps are rife with disgusting insects, but I never imagined any would be this blatant! You can't talk your way out of this! Only death awaits!"

Your classic emotionally unstable stalker.

Not to validate her actions, but anyone would be pissed seeing the love of their life being groped in their underwear. The real root of all this strife was the teeny grandma.

Kikyou was certainly rattled by the sheer aggression behind the attacks, but she was agile enough to avoid the belt, barely.

Selen's assault showed no signs of relenting. The cursed belt sliced through the air with a series of sharp cracks.

Stuck in the middle of this combat zone, Lloyd's eyes were slowly beginning to open.

"Um, what's going…?"

"DIEEEEEEEEEEEE!"

Both ends of the belt reached past Lloyd's sides like tentacles, trying to grab Kikyou.

"Argh, I almost had it, too!"

Kikyou whipped a blade out of her pocket and attempted to nail the belt to a wooden stool. There was a satisfying *thunk* as the weapon was pinned, but it was an artifact made from the skin of the Divine Beast Vritra, which meant it could not be stopped that easily.

"Hmph!"

A surge of power ran outward from Selen's waist, and the knife went flying. Then the belt wrapped itself around Kikyou.

"Crap! …No other way out."

With a painful grimace, Kikyou began contorting herself. There were several creepy pops, and then she slipped free of the constriction. Seemed like she'd dislocated several joints to escape.

"How the—?" Selen gasped.

Kikyou took advantage of that opening. Instead of running, she leaped forward, getting in close. The moment she was in range, she grabbed Selen's waist and threw her into a suplex.

Hitting the back of one's head on hard pavement would spell bad news.

"…Did I get her? Huh? Seriously?!"

But Selen was unharmed. The cursed belt had formed a cushion, protecting her skull.

"I've had bad experiences being thrown around before… Now, die!"

As if it were nothing, Selen righted herself and renewed her onslaught.

"Wh-who is this monster?!"

Was it even possible to get away from her? As Kikyou began looking for an escape route…

"So this is what a proper massage looks like!" Lloyd exclaimed, sounding very impressed. "You have to hit the back of the head like that, huh."

He was still in his underwear.

"You stay back, Sir Lloyd!"

Now that he'd attracted Selen's attention, though, she couldn't stop stealing peeks through the steam at his body. She was no longer remotely focused on the fight.

Oh, now's my chance!

Kikyou couldn't miss this opportunity! With that, she turned and sprinted away.

"Huh? She left," Lloyd observed, confused.

Selen came racing over to him.

"Sir Lloyd! What's going on here? How did you end up in your underwear?!"

His eyes weren't down there.

"Uh, well, she works here with me and was showing me how to do a proper massage."

"I don't see how that follows, but in any case, you're covered in some weird balm! We'd better go rest in that shop while I wipe you off."

Not once taking her eyes off his nether regions, Selen led him to a nearby rest area, without allowing him to dress that she might continue feasting her eyes…

Lloyd, meanwhile, was studiously turning the "proper massage" he'd just witnessed over in his mind and missed his chance to put on his clothes.

"I see… So that's a real massage… You do this, then…uh, Selen? I'm still not dressed…"

Selen just kept pushing him toward the food/souvenir stand. They sold everything from cypress handicrafts to little household tools to packs of vegetables that grew wild in the mountains.

The pair took a seat in the restaurant, greeted by the aroma coming from the oven: a flatbread with cheese on it, very similar to pizza. Families were chattering all around them.

Any restaurant with a dress code would have turned a boy in his underwear and a girl with a cursed belt writhing around her waist away at the door.

They certainly got stares.

"Mom, look!"

"Shh, don't stare."

Selen paid these interactions no heed. Lloyd was embarrassed by his lack of clothing but nevertheless sat down in an empty seat across from her.

"Uh...I'd really like to put something on..."

"Let me wipe you down first, Sir Lloyd."

Without missing a beat, she took the moist towelettes the restaurant provided and used them to wipe Lloyd all over—painstakingly, as if polishing a beloved treasure.

"Um, Selen? That balm is dry now, so I don't think we need to be so thorough..."

"But you can't put a tux on over this! You borrowed it, right?"

"Urp...right, I can't get it dirty. The cleaning fees will be astronomical..."

Even in this tourist trap in his underwear, Lloyd was worried about laundry, like the good housewife he was.

Now that she had found his weakness, Selen smiled, taking on the air of a car enthusiast hand-washing her newest acquisition.

"Oh, I'm out of wet wipes...Waiter! Bring another dozen!"

The waiter would probably never hear such an absurd request again in his lifetime. It took him by surprise, but he caught the threat in Selen's gaze and dashed into the storeroom.

While Selen waited for the delivery, someone crept up behind her.

"You seem to be in trouble. Would you like to use my moist towelette?"

"Why, thank you! Sir Lloyd, let us contin— *Yow!* Those are hot!"

Selen had accepted without even glancing at the person offering, but the wet wipe proved so hot, she was left yelping in an entirely un-Selen-like fashion.

"Hey! What's the big idea? Who makes wet wipes this hot?"

"We aren't that kind of shop, so please refrain from inappropriate behavior."

Selen whipped around to protest and found Riho looming over her, eyes like daggers, fire magic wreathed around her mithril arm. She was clearly quite worked up herself.

"Oh...R-Riho..."

"Riho!"

"You seem to be enjoying yourself, m'lady. While I was busy sweeping horse poop."

Riho plopped down in a chair, and when the waiter arrived with armfuls of wet towels, she ordered a coffee.

"Just how did you talk him into something this freaky? How'd he get covered in goo on a date?"

Riho glared at the pile of moist towelettes and the balm still clearly visible on Lloyd's skin.

"This wasn't me! It was the hand of destiny! Some weird woman began smearing oil all over Lloyd's body!"

"A weird woman other than you?"

"How weird do you think I am?!"

Selen Hemein was a military cadet, yet the military police already had her on their watch list. For being a stalker.

"So why are you in your underwear, Lloyd? Another outbreak of Selen-ness?" Riho asked, rubbing her temples.

Lloyd shook his head. "No, I just wanted to learn what a proper massage was like."

"Well, that explains it," Riho said, instantly convinced.

"This is a very strange conversation!" Selen remarked. "Riho, you're usually not one to give in so easily!"

Selen offered a sound argument, a rarity, but Riho's serious expression never wavered.

"No, Lloyd is duty-bound to learn what a normal massage is as soon as possible."

"What kind of duty is *that*? That's a *very* loaded statement!"

While Selen and Riho argued, Lloyd finished wiping himself and put the tux back on.

"Sorry… Now that I'm finally a military cadet, I can't exactly let myself get arrested."

"How would a massage get you arrested?" Selen looked from Lloyd to Riho, then gave up and sat down.

"You're better off not knowing," Riho said, sipping her coffee. "Anyway, I'm on break, so I figured I'd touch base. You notice anything weird?"

"Yes, being in Lloyd's arms is very warm."

The bitter look on Riho's face was likely unrelated to the quality of her coffee.

"…Must I remind you of the goal here?"

"Clinching the deal with Sir Lloyd!…Uh, and the people-in-comas thing."

"What a beautiful smile on the first half. Well, as long as you remember, we'll call it good."

Riho clearly had a soft spot for her. She turned to Lloyd next.

"But you're the main deal here. Notice anything?"

"Uh…well…"

"No matter how small. It might be a clue."

"Hmm. Well, there's more people in short sleeves."

"Yeah, it's getting warmer out." Riho looked like she was getting a headache.

"Sorry, Sir Lloyd and I were just enjoying our date so much."

It would be more accurate to say Selen was sole member of this trio having the time of her life. Deciding she was in for the long haul, Riho ordered another cup of coffee.

"So I'm the only one who actually did *any* investigating?"

"You found something out, Riho?!" Lloyd asked, beaming at her across the table.

Riho hid her blush behind the coffee.

"That's how you earn trust, m'lady," she said triumphantly.

"Hngg," Selen groaned. "You're sure you've got a lead?"

Riho nodded, taking a scrap of paper out of her pocket.

"First, the guest in 102. He reserved a suite but canceled at the last minute—gave a weird excuse about not liking the suite name. This was before Allan collapsed."

"That's odd… Was the suite named Riho?"

"If it was Selen, that *would* explain it."

They glared at each other.

"…Next, the people staying in 201. They're ordering an insane amount of food. But there are only two of them. People are wondering if they're feeding something voracious."

"Like a monster?"

"Bingo. Even if it's just a pet, that's against the rules. Our hotel requires a proper cage and an additional fee, as well as the use of a room designated for that purpose."

Riho was clearly embracing her new role as a hotel employee.

"Wow, Riho," Lloyd said, his trust rocketing even higher. "You were born to do this job."

"Mercenaries work all kinds of places. Experience talks."

"Hmm," Selen said, fixing her with a suspicious glare. "That does sound significant…assuming it's *true*."

"What, you don't believe it, m'lady? The hotel rules clearly state—"

"Not the rules. The rumors. They could be exaggerations, lies, or distortions. Until we see it with our own eyes…"

Selen's gaze made it clear that no matter what the facts were, she'd find something to complain about to lower Riho's skyrocketing reputation.

"Ha-ha-ha," Riho chuckled, as if she'd been waiting for this. "Then let's go check it out together! Time to quit pretending you're going to get married."

"Huh? Quit?"

"Of course! Why would prospective marriage partners be investigating the suspects' rooms? Look, I admit half of this is just wanting you to share my pain…"

"...And you've baited me into this."

For once, Riho had the advantage, and all Selen could do was grumble.

"Right. With that settled, let's get back to the hotel. Oh, and, m'lady, we're going to approach these suspects as maids, so you'll have to ditch that dress."

"Argh, fine. If this means Sir Lloyd and I can work together, it might prove valuable practice at maintaining a relationship on the job, so...I'll stay positive."

"That much positivity will get you thrown in jail someday, m'lady."

Consider the earlier statement redacted—Selen's power to make anything about Lloyd meant she *always* had the advantage.

Riho and Selen were decked out in cream-colored dresses and white aprons. Lloyd followed them in his bellboy uniform, pushing a cleaning cart.

Unlike the hall on the floor of suites, this corridor was plain, with few decorations. At the end of it was room 102.

Riho ran over the plan once more, keeping her voice low.

"First, m'lady and I will enter to make the bed."

"And if he tries to run or harm the two of you, I'll jump in from behind."

"And after Sir Lloyd saves me, the two of us will inevitably—"

Seemed like one of them was running an entirely different operation.

"Ignore her words and her entire existence. Lloyd, you hide in the hall and keep watch."

"Er, uh...I-I'll do my best..."

Selen's remark had confused him, and he was now looking rather tense.

"Oh, Sir Lloyd...here? In the hall! So daring!"

"Wrap it up, m'lady."

Riho rubbed her knuckles on Selen's head and yanked her cheeks until she returned to reality.

"I'm ready to go! I have seen the future and have a clear plan of action! Time to make dreams come true!" Selen said, sounding like an ad for a new real estate development.

"As long as you're motivated," Riho muttered. She was used to it by now.

Focusing, she stepped up to the door…and knocked.

"Housekeeping," she called.

There was a moment's silence, and then the door opened.

Inside stood a young man with even features and a deep tan, dressed in a T-shirt, baggy pants, and hiking boots. With this outfit and his wiry build, he looked like a backpacker, or at least someone with a very active job.

"Mm? What?" he inquired, piercing eyes looking from Riho to Selen.

"We're here to make your bed," Riho announced, giving no hint of their true purpose.

The man ran a hand through his hair, rumpling it.

"Weird…I don't remember asking."

"Sorry, we're new here…Well, since we're here anyway, we're happy to—"

Selen tried to look past him. The man put his hand to his chin, thinking, studying her face.

"So you really want to come in and clean?"

"Uh, yes," Selen said, confused by the question. Riho was swearing inside.

"I see, I see…I get it." He grinned at them.

"G-get what?"

Tension rose between them.

"You two…?" he started.

Crap, we're made! Riho started to shift her weight to signal Lloyd.

"…have passion!"

""Huh?""

Grinning broadly, the man threw his thumbs up, excitement in his voice. Neither Selen nor Riho had seen this coming, and they both failed to hide their surprise. The man didn't seem to care, though. He just nodded and began babbling.

"You got the wrong room! But you still want to make the bed! You want to polish your skills and make a career of this! You love cleaning beyond all measure! Gushing sweat! Burning fervor! I love passionate people!"

"Er, yeah...well..."

The "gushing sweat" comment seemed particularly dubious, but this dude wasn't about to let them get a word in edgewise.

"But I'm afraid my room just isn't that dirty... I know! I'll go mess it up for you! Hold that sweat a moment!" He gave them a quick bow and vanished into his room.

Everyone stood frozen for a moment; then Riho yelped.

"He got us!"

"Wh-what? Why are you yelling?" Selen asked, looking like she was afraid Riho had caught the man's enthusiasm.

Riho shook her head, grimacing. "He's gone to destroy the evidence! Unless he's *really* stupid. I mean, who goes to mess their own room up?"

But before she could say anything else, the tanned hunk came back grinning so broadly, his teeth gleamed.

"Welcome! I messed it up for you, rookie maids! I've never deliberately messed up a room before! It's harder than I thought! Man! Sweat! Gushing!"

"He *is* really stupid!"

Riho and Selen looked at him the way you would a particularly dumb dog.

At this point, Lloyd peered around the corner and, with a start, stepped forward.

He gave the man a long, searching look. "...Shouma?"

The man blinked and spun around to face Lloyd.

"Mm? Hmm? Wait...*Lloyd?!*"

Certain now, Lloyd broke into a huge smile, throwing his arms around the older boy.

"Wow! Shouma, it's been way too long!"

Shouma hugged Lloyd back, rubbing his head. "Lloyd! You've grown so tall!"

Like two close-knit brothers reunited.

"Uh, what? You know each other?" Riho asked.

"Yeah, this is Shouma. He's from Kunlun."

"""...Oh."""

Both girls let out a little yelp of horror. After experiencing Alka's superhuman powers and outlandish behavior, well...it certainly explained a lot about Shouma.

"Shouma brings stuff from outside Kunlun back to the village."

"I transport goods, collect info, look into the latest fads—all part of my job. So what's up, Lloyd? You working here now?"

"Just for the weekend. I'm actually a cadet in the army in Azami."

Shouma immediately began rubbing his cheek on Lloyd.

"Wow! Your dream came true! Such passion! Passion in action! Congrats, Lloyd!"

His cries echoed down the hall. People were leaning out of their rooms to see what the fuss was about.

"Er, um...sorry, we're bothering the other guests," Riho said, but Shouma just kept yelling.

"Ohhh! Sorry! Sorry! Okay! We've got a lot to catch up on, so—my room!"

"You're sure?"

"Of course I am! We gotta enjoy this...once the room is clean!"

Shouma proudly ushered them all in, only to get looks of horror.

The place looked like it had been burgled. Clothes had been flung everywhere.

"So you two are Lloyd's classmates? Such passion!" Shouma cried.

"Yeah..."

What exactly was passionate about that? Neither of them could keep up with this dude.

Neatly folding shirts, Lloyd asked the obvious question.

"Wait, but why are you staying here?"

"On a delivery!" Shouma said. "That's what brought me."

"Oh, so you're working?"

"Yeah, some pretty dangerous goods...like three cases of bottle bombs. Really urgent stuff! They must have something they really wanna burn! Gotta support that kinda passion! It really got me right here, you know? So I figured they should blow up extra good and brought bottle bombs modified with magic stones! The fire will be massive!"

"Bottle bombs?" Selen remarked. "How terrifying."

"Don't look away!" Riho said. "You're the one who ordered them, right?"

Obviously.

Oblivious to their exchange, Shouma kept right on talking. Evidently, he wasn't a detail-oriented dude.

"Then I figured, why not try a suite? But it was named after a real creep, so I was like, ew, sorry, can I change rooms? I'd have had nightmares staying there."

"...So you're rich?" Selen asked.

"Money has no value," Shouma declared. "Not to me, anyway."

Riho frowned at this. "You're from Kunlun, but you don't *look* strong."

"Oh, yeah, well, you gotta learn to hide your aura, right? Otherwise, anyone's who's been through some real shit or some martial artists looking for a challenge will pick up on it and hassle you. Also..."

He shot both girls a sharp look.

"People try to take advantage of us."

For a moment...just a moment, they caught a glimpse of unfathomable power, and a chill ran down their spines.

They gulped.

He laughed. "Sorry! Sorry! Didn't mean to scare you! Just...lots of history. Ah-ha-ha. I can tell from looking at Lloyd that you two ain't the type."

Even his smile seemed frightening now.

"What are you talking about, Shouma?" Lloyd asked, behind him.

"Nah, nothing! Right! All clean! Well, it's a shame, but we'd better wrap things up quick. Don't wanna run into anyone who might be tagging after you, Lloyd."

"Like who?"

Shouma gave Lloyd a head rub to avoid answering. "Lemme ask you one thing, Lloyd. You still love that novel?"

"Yes! Still my favorite. I reread it all the time."

"That's all I need to hear! See you around! And you two—look after Lloyd for me."

With that, he shouldered his luggage and was gone like the wind.

"...What's with that guy?"

"For a moment there, his eyes... Augh, I don't wanna think about it."

Lloyd was just pleased to have met his brother figure, but the two girls felt like they'd brushed up against the unknowable.

Still reeling from their surprise encounter with the Kunlun villager, Lloyd's group went to check on the other suspicious guests.

"Get it together... There's still the highly suspicious room 201."

This time, they were wheeling a cart full of food.

"They're the ones ordering all the food, right?" Selen asked.

Riho nodded. "Yeah, I checked the receipts, and the volume is straight-up insane. Far more than two people could possibly eat. Which means..."

"There's someone...some*thing* else in there."

"We have to assume they're hiding something they don't want anyone else seeing."

They nodded gravely. Then, a hesitant voice rose from the cart in front of them.

"Um...so what should I...?"

They'd hidden Lloyd inside the cart. Riho bent down, whispering to him.

"You're a backup plan—if they're too cautious to let us in the room, we can leave the cart behind."

"And I can check the interior for anything suspicious!"

"Yes, you're great at remaining undetected, Sir Lloyd! This will be easy for you."

"Oh, everyone in the village can do what I do!" Lloyd said sheepishly.

"When I played hide-and-seek with the other village children, I could never find anybody!"

The girls smiled, but those smiles were very strained.

"Yeah, by the standards of your village..."

"I never imagined they'd be hiding so far belowground they were under the bedrock!"

Did that even count as hide-and-seek anymore? What passed for common sense in Kunlun was a constant source of astonishment.

Feeling like nothing could surprise them after hearing Lloyd's tales, Riho and Selen reached the door to room 201 and nodded at each other.

"Right..."

They knocked, then waited. Footsteps like an excited child's raced toward the door.

"A kid?" Riho wondered, baffled.

When the door was flung open, a familiar blond girl stepped out.

"Welcome! Nothing better than a meal you can expense! My favorite food is meat someone else is paying for! Free meals are better than three meals! Ya got the goods, Johnny? Don't think you can pull one over on Mena Quinone— Wait, Riho and Selen?"

This stream of words came from the older sister of their classmate Phyllo—Mena.

Riho and Selen stared at her in surprise—but that soon gave way to puzzled frowns.

"Who's Johnny?"

"We're not Johnny!"

Mena winced. "I'm afraid I've let you catch a rare glimpse of me disgracing myself."

"Nah, you're pretty much always like that."

Mena Quinone had gold hair and smiling eyes, and she was currently a Royal Sorcerer. Words tumbled out of her like an announcer at a pro wrestling event, but she was a first-rate expert in water magic. Thanks to Lloyd, they'd realized her goofy exterior was a cover for a much more calculating interior.

"So why are you here? Seasonal work?"

"Something like that… Let's not talk in the hall. Let's go in and sit down!"

"Hey, that's for me to offer! But I guess you two are safe."

Safe for what? Riho and Selen looked at each other.

"What's that mean? You don't have a monster hiding in here, do you?"

"…A monster would be cuter. Nah, I guess she's cute in her own way."

A cold sweat on her brow, Mena beckoned them in.

"……Hic."

Phyllo was leaning against the wall. Her face was expressionless—but bright red. Bits and pieces of the furniture appeared to have been demolished.

"Er, Phyllo?"

If Mena was here, it made sense Phyllo would be with her. But with her face that red…she must have been *drunk*. A fact that made Riho start backing away.

"……Mm?……Riho……Selen?" Phyllo's head tilted to one side.

Selen chose her words carefully. "Um…Phyllo? Why are you…?"

"……Wait……I wanna roll around…"

Phyllo threw herself on a bed, wrapped her arms around a pillow, and proceeded to roll back and forth.

"…Talking to her seems imposs— Yikes!"

Phyllo's rolling had abruptly transformed into a throwing technique known as the Hell Wheel. The pillow tore apart, scattering the stuffing everywhere. If the pillow had been a person, neither of them would have been able to eat offal of any kind ever again.

"……Not enough joints."

With that sinister statement, Phyllo leaned against the wall again.

"What the hell was *that*? Explain!" Riho snarled.

Mena just shook her head. "Uh, I got a little carried away and ordered some booze, and Phyllo accidentally drank some… Once she's full, she'll fall asleep, so I've been ordering everything I can."

All that food was just going into Phyllo, then? The solution to the mystery left them dumbfounded.

"......Mm?...... Riho......Selen?"

"Y-yeah, Phyllo. You feeling better?"

"......Wait...... I wanna roll around..."

"Is it me, or is she repeating the same conversation?"

Phyllo grabbed a nearby chair and began rolling around. This time, she shifted into an Octopus Hold, and soon the chair was a pile of kindling.

"......Not enough creaking bones."

She reassumed her default position against the wall, with a statement arguably even more sinister.

"That...doesn't appear to be getting better. More like she's powering up."

"She's a growing girl?"

"She's tall enough right now!"

"......Mm?...... Riho......Selen?"

"Is this gonna end without bloodshed?"

The infinite loop was starting again, but just as the three of them clutched their heads...Phyllo did something else.

She began looking right and left, sniffing the air.

Was this the start of a new loop?

Then Phyllo stopped dead in her tracks, whispering, "...........I smell my master."

"""Ah!"""

Only now did they remember Lloyd was on standby under the cart.

"Lloyd's here?" Mena asked.

Riho nodded, glancing at the cart.

"...Only he can stop Phyllo now."

"But if we put Lloyd in front of her, they'll grapple so hard, he may not emerge with his purity unscathed."

"Please. If this room gets any more wrecked, I can't expense it."

Riho found it hard to believe Mena's account could cover the damages now, but...

"No! If we feed this ravenous beast bloody meat...the results will be far too scandalous!"

Riho found it hard to see the difference between that scenario and Selen's own behavior.

"I get your point, Selen, but talking about it isn't getting us anywhere...not that I'm a fan of the idea..."

"Oh no!"

As they talked, Phyllo had gotten down on all fours and was rapidly approaching the cart.

She sniffed at it, expressionless. Like a police dog searching for drugs, she smelled the cart from every angle and then peered underneath.

"Uh, hi...," Lloyd said, waving weakly.

"...Welcome."

Then Phyllo grabbed his wrist and dragged him onto the bed.

"Ph-Phyllooo!"

No sooner was Lloyd on the bed than she was mounted on top of him.

"...Your fault for letting your guard down."

"I'm not letting my..."

"...Your *what*?"

"My guard down!"

Their conversation wasn't quite adding up. It was as if one was perceiving a double entendre where none existed. Like a scene in a rom-com.

""Hmph.""

Picking up on that vibe, Selen and Riho snorted in unison. Both were looking extremely cross.

"Phyllo's drunk. Cut her some slack," Mena said.

"So drunks can do whatever they want?!" Selen pounced. "That makes no sense! The law does not agree!"

Riho would normally point out that stalkers shouldn't be discussing the law, but instead she went full-on dark hero. "Then in the law's stead, I shall pass judgment..."

It was kinda badass.

Meanwhile, Lloyd was being further dominated.

"...Listen to that creaking." Phyllo had locked his joints, listening to the sound of his bones.

"Hey! My bones! They're—"

But before Lloyd could say another word, she wrapped her legs around his and went into a spin, throwing him behind her—a perfect Hell Wheel.

Lloyd was not so easily bested. Even as he spun, he said, "Hang on a second!"

"...Hi-yah!" Phyllo threw her arms around him from behind.

With love...she put him into a perfect Octopus Hold.

This involved a strangle hold, entirely cutting off the flow of oxygen to the brain. Anyone else would have gone purple, but...

"Phyllo! You're pressing up against me!" Lloyd turned red instead, mortified. Guess what was pressing up against him. Hint: something spanning thirty-five inches.

"...Not enough for you, Master? Then..."

And finally, Phyllo put her legs around Lloyd's face.

""".....gh!"""

Selen and Riho let out a wordless shriek.

"Mmph! Mmmph...," Lloyd protested.

Phyllo toppled over, slamming Lloyd to the ground headfirst.

There was a loud *thunk*—not a sound you'd expect to come from a bed.

"...Only you can handle my full strength, Master. *Yawn...*"

A wave of sleepiness seemed to hit Phyllo. Her eyes fluttered, and she flopped over on the bed.

Lying upside-down where she'd dropped him after the storm of violence, Lloyd was speechless.

"...What a nice dream... *Mmph...*," Phyllo mumbled.

The preceding scene would have been fatal to anyone else, so it was more of a nightmare, really.

But Phyllo looked satisfied. Sprawled out on the bed, she was soon fast asleep. His clothes and hair all messed up, Lloyd flapped his lips as if to protest...but it was too late.

"So much physical contact! Unforgivable!"

"You could have taken his place," Riho told Selen.

"And died?"

Selen definitely would have.

"Yeah, no normal person could take Phyllo's Hell Wheel-turned-Octopus Sleeper-turned-Avalanche Brainbuster! Well done, Lloyd."

"Don't ever let her drink again."

Mena settled down on the floor since there were no chairs intact.

From the bed, Lloyd broached the real question. "So why are the two of you here?"

"Oh, see, the government asked us to investigate a thing."

"You mean…?"

"They've been finding people unconscious, like the life's been drained out of them."

They hadn't been expecting to hear this from Mena. She didn't seem to notice.

"So I took advantage of Phyllo's school holiday and brought her with me," Mena explained. "Naturally, once we got here, the first task at hand was to expense a bunch of good grub."

"You say that like it's common sense."

"But this means our goals are aligned."

Riho filled Mena in on their side—stressing the injustice of being forced to work while Selen got to fulfill her dreams.

"I guess I can see how we'd be suspicious… My bad."

"Would you be up for comparing notes? Anything you know that we don't?"

"Hmm… Well, the pizza and ice cream here are amazing."

"Not about the local delicacies! About the case! I wanna solve this thing so I can go back to being a guest on vacation! Before the holiday ends!"

"That pizza was very good," Selen said sorrowfully. "But anything would taste good eaten with Sir Lloyd."

"Argh, and this while I was sweeping up horse dung!"

Before the conversation could get any more sidetracked, Mena shared the intel the government had provided.

"The incidents started about two years ago. A number of adventurers and hunters were found in the forest, the life drained out of them, leaving them comatose for three days and nights. So an investigation was launched. At first, they just figured it was a monster of some kind and didn't take it that seriously...but then, something happened that turned it into a huge problem."

"What was that?"

"Illegal cultivation...of highly dangerous monsters called treants."

"What? Treants are monsters? There were tons of those all around the village, and just the other day..."

"... *What?*" Mena shouted, her eyes opening briefly.

"Ignore him, Mena. Go on!"

"Well, uh...you've heard treants can be turned into lumber? Someone's cultivating them illegally, hoping to get rich quick. And this time, they might have a seedling."

"A seedling?"

Mina proceeded to fill them in on what made the saplings so dangerous.

"Yeah, and seedlings can spread faster than the seeds. It was stolen from a lab somewhere...and whoever's been growing treants from the seeds might be using the seedling now."

"So if that expands them into a horde... Crap."

"Lots of details are still murky, so I brought Phyllo with me, calling it a vacation...but maybe it's a good thing there's really something to it. Now I can rack up the expenses guilt-free!"

"That's all you care about, huh," Riho said, disgusted.

Mena let her eyes slowly open, speaking seriously again. "On the off chance there *is* a seedling involved, we've got a shot at winning. With that lake nearby, I've got a lot more options for my water magic... Even if they've laid down roots and are expanding fast, I should be able to handle it."

"At least you're on top of it."

"It *is* my job...but having fun is a key part of any work!" Mena was back to her usual tone. "Now that I've got me some powerful allies on the hotel staff, we'd better get this thing cranking!"

"All right! I wanna get this over with and kick back, too."

Riho got up…

But Mena's focus was already off-track.

"To the restaurant!"

"That's what you mean? Didn't you already have enough food?"

"Phyllo ate most of that! Like sixty percent of it!"

"That's basically half!"

"And with Phyllo all drunk, I don't feel like I really ate anything. I can't fight on an empty stomach! We've gotta fill up before any combat happens."

"Geez… Don't I have enough headaches to wrangle?" Riho muttered. It was almost a prayer.

But that prayer…would never be answered. She had forgotten that the biggest headache was still out there.

Back at the shop on the East Side, a fruitless battle was beginning.

"What does this mean, Marie?!"

"What do you mean?"

It was evening. With Lloyd gone, Marie was glumly drinking coffee while Alka stood on the table, her entire body shaking with rage like a little dancer.

Or maybe something weirder than that. It was like a video game character glitching. Marie just gave the half-grown grandma her best frosty stare.

"Why didn't you tell me, Marie?"

"Tell you what?"

It took nearly an hour for Alka to return to normal. When she finally calmed down, she explained herself.

"Hff. Hff… The place Lloyd's working…I didn't think it would be *there*!"

She waved a flyer around. It was beautifully printed, explaining the facilities available at the Reiyoukaku Hotel and in its vicinity.

"What about it? Seemed perfectly ordinary to me."

"Look closely! Right here!" Alka was pointing to an illustration of the hotel staff bowing and smiling.

"A drawing of a smile?"

"Not that! What's wrong with your eyes?" Alka drew a circle on the flyer with her finger.

"...The bellboy...uniform?" Marie asked.

"Ding! Ding! Ding! Ding!" Alka yelled, as if Marie had correctly answered a question on a game show. "Exactly!"

Marie was clutching her head now.

That's right! She fed Lloyd novels about heroic soldiers as a kid just so she could see him in a military uniform!

The contrast between Lloyd's cute smile and the stoic uniform really did it for Alka. Her fetish was borderline pathological. This was another symptom of that illness.

"A once-in-a-lifetime chance to see him in this uniform! A matter of life and death! How could I let this chance go to waste, you loathsome nincompoop?!"

"........."

"Lloyd in this uniform! Leading me to my room, carrying my things, saying, 'Watch your step!' Just the thought of it, and... Augh! Augh!"

"........."

Marie finished her coffee and went to the kitchen to fill the cup with water. Like she'd promised Lloyd she would.

Alka was now bleating like a goat. Marie smiled at her.

"Shall we?"

"Augh... Mm?"

"You want to see Lloyd's uniform, right?"

"But Lloyd told you not to go, right? You're sure?"

"Lloyd mistakenly believes I'm the hero saving this kingdom from the shadows."

Time for a quick recap: Lloyd wasn't aware that Marie was a princess. One misunderstanding after another had led him to the conclusion that she was the kingdom's secret savior.

"Oh, right, he did say that…," Alka muttered, then shot Marie a *So what?* look.

Marie proudly explained her plan.

"Suppose there was a dangerous criminal in that hotel. Wouldn't that give us an excuse to be there? And once the danger's gone, since we're there anyway, we might as well enjoy the hot springs. Pretty good, right?"

Alka grinned. "You've become a very bad girl, Marie… Hmm?"

Marie had climbed up on Alka's back.

"Right, let's go! It's a quick trip for anyone from Kunlun! We'll be seeing Lloyd in no time!"

"I'm not your personal carriage!" Alka shrieked.

"According to tradition, witches grant wishes in exchange for payment of equal value," Marie replied calmly. "In other words, your payment for seeing Lloyd in a bellboy uniform is that you have to carry *me* there with you."

"Like student, like master… I dunno whether to be horrified or proud."

"Hi-ho! Giddyap!"

Riho had unwittingly jinxed herself. Further headaches were on the way.

"Before anything awful happens! Before disaster strikes!"

"Or so we're claiming, right?"

A disaster? Little did they know, their excuse was realer than either of them suspected.

While the overprotective duo were racing toward them at blinding speed, Lloyd and company were headed for the hotel restaurant.

The restaurant was hugely popular with hotel guests and visitors alike. It allowed them to enjoy a meal with a lovely view of the lake.

Coba was standing at the entrance, greeting guests with a broad smile.

"A personal welcome from the owner?" Lloyd said, impressed. "He sure works hard."

"Oh, Lloyd!" Coba cried, hustling over to them. "Sorry about all this… How's it going?"

"Still searching for clues," Lloyd reported apologetically.

"Well, I don't need the culprit caught immediately," Coba said cheerily. "What matters is that you stay on guard against anyone else falling victim."

"Thank you for your kind words, sir!"

Lloyd bowed politely. Selen appeared at his side.

"And our meeting is going swimmingly! Not only will no one see through the ruse—at this rate, we'll really end up married!"

She was definitely benefiting the most from this arrangement. What had happened to that whole conflict with her father, anyway?

"Uh, sure… Glad to hear it's going well," Coba managed to say. Then he noticed their uniforms. "Mm? You're going to eat in the restaurant dressed like that?"

"Is that a problem?"

Coba scratched his hairless head. "Well, it's not the staff dining area… Yeah, better not go in wearing those uniforms. Do you mind changing? Also, Allan's and Selen's families are inside, so…"

"Ugh," Riho groaned.

But Selen was still going full throttle. "We can't get caught! We'll have to keep the date going! Friends, let us celebrate our inevitable marriage! That's our excuse for dining here! Come!"

"It really doesn't have to be *this* restaurant…," Riho grumbled.

Mena giggled. "Wow, it's like you can't bear seeing Lloyd and Selen flirting even if you *know* it's just pretend."

"That's not it!" Riho insisted. "Just…my point is…"

Words failed her when something hit too close to home.

"Cool, then go change! This restaurant's so good, they put it in the hotel guide."

"Y-yeah… Looking forward to it! Dammit."

"…Geez. Wouldn't it be easier to just admit it?" Mena gave Riho a look of pity, but Riho stuck to her guns. Coba patted her on the shoulder.

"Looking forward to it… Owner? What is it?"

"Since you're looking forward to it, I hate to ask, but…we're short-staffed…"

"……Seriously?" Riho froze, her mouth open.

"Well, Riho! Sir Lloyd and I will just go change, so get some work done while you wait!"

Triumphantly, Selen turned and left.

"…To hell with horses!" Riho spat, trudging off to the kitchen.

As the sun set, the magic stones began lighting up. In the restaurant in Reiyoukaku, Lloyd and Selen sat in formal attire, gazing at the view of the lake—well, at least one of them was.

"You're wonderful…"

"Er, yeah…Selen…"

"Tch… Tch… Tch!"

Riho's tongue clicks were basically their background music.

"How many children should we have? I'd like enough to form a platoon!"

"You've forgotten the engagement and skipped ahead to the honeymoon!"

Riho angrily slammed a glass of water down in front of Selen, forcing her to wipe up the spray with a napkin.

"Honestly, where does this hotel get their servers?"

"You'll pay for that later," Riho barked. Then she saw Lloyd looking confused. "Hang in there, Lloyd."

"Come, come! Bring us our feast!" Selen demanded. She'd clearly forgotten all about the crimes they were investigating. "I'll feed you, Sir Lloyd! Open wide!"

"I'll tear you wide open!" Riho snarled, glaring.

Lloyd quickly grabbed her hand. "Riho…over there…"

She followed his gaze and saw Threonine and Selen's father talking. Desperate to catch a lead in the case, Threonine was raining questions down on his opponent as if conducting an interrogation. He seemed ready to tempt him with food for a confession, like they were on a police show.

"Argh..."

It wouldn't do to blow their cover. Riho caught Lloyd's meaning and reluctantly nodded. Selen pulled his arm closer, looking proud of herself.

"I think this lowly server should hurry up and fetch our meal, don't you, darling?"

"You little... Fine."

Then the picturesque view of the illuminated lake outside the window...was suddenly decorated with two familiar faces. One was a pip-squeak of a grandma with two black pigtails. The other wore a witch's black pointed hat.

When Riho's eyes met theirs, they hastily hid themselves.

"...I just...saw the witch and your chief..."

Selen froze for a moment but quickly recovered. "Heh...heh-heh. Idle threats will get you nowhere, Riho."

"No, I didn't mean... Maybe I'm just tired." Riho rubbed her eyes.

"I'm so hungry!" Mena wailed, like a petulant child.

She was the oldest person there.

"...Yeah, I must be tired. With everything that's happened, how could anyone *not* be?"

Riho's shoulders drooped, and she headed back to the kitchen. All manner of utensils dangled from the ceiling, and the ingredients were top-notch. Riho figured she'd bring out a salad or something...but then noticed something amiss.

"Weird... There's no one here."

At this hour, the place should have been teeming. Riho looked again.

"What say we mix in some of this balm-based puree? It smells positively poisonous."

"Good idea, Marie. This soup should drive off the pests."

"I'll give it a good stir."

"Oh, you really know how to stir a pot! Like a regular witch."

"I *am* a witch! Hee-hee-hee!"

They were *clearly* up to no good.

"What the hell are you two doing?"

The two idiots spun around. Their eyes said it all—Lloyd deprivation had driven them around the bend. Riho had seen that look before…in Selen's eyes. A sad state of affairs.

"Oh, Riho! We're making soup," Marie said, without a trace of guilt.

"A delicious soup that will destroy that interloper Selen's very mind," Alka cackled. She showed Riho the contents of the pot. The color made her dry-heave.

"Uh…there are other guests here, so please don't… You're disrupting business."

"What? I'm sure this will taste marvelous," Marie insisted.

"I heard you say 'poisonous' just a second ago!" Riho snapped. "Go on. Try some."

"Er…"

"It's delicious, right? You said so yourself! Surely you're confident in your own creation, Chef Marie."

"…Uh…" Marie couldn't think of a good retort.

"Good luck, Marie!" Alka threw her under the bus.

"………" Marie hadn't expected to have to try any herself, but she reluctantly raised a spoon to her lips. "…Here goes nothing."

Slurp. (The sweet sound of soup being inhaled.)

Splat. (The sickly sound of the same soup being violently spat out.)

"Tolerable," Marie announced, wiping her mouth.

"Liar!" Riho yelped.

"'E f'avor ith rewwy lingering in my mouf," Marie added. She'd never make it as a food critic.

"Your entire tongue's gone numb! We can't serve this! They'll shut the place down! And what did you do with the real cooks?"

"When we got here, there was only one weird lady," Alka said. "A suspicious redhead. She was trying to do something with that bottle of balm."

"Mm? Redhead?"

Riho felt like someone had been talking about a redhead earlier...but before she could piece it together, Marie stole a peek at the dining hall.

"...Master, Riho, look here."

They did and saw...

"Yes, darling. Open wide!"

"Um, Selen... That's just water. Eep!"

"See? That's what happens when you don't do it properly. I spilled it on your pants. Let me wipe them for you."

"Er, I can do that myself! Seriously!"

"""".............."""""

Thunk.

"Thanks for waiting! Chef's special soup."

"It rea'y does th' body good."

"I reckon you ought to savor it like water after the apocalypse."

Health code violations be damned! Riho had slammed the slop down in front of Selen, Marie and Alka grinning on either side of her.

Their unexpected arrival clearly flummoxed Selen. "Oh...my! Where'd you come from?"

"Chief...and Marie?"

"Explanations can wait. First—m'lady, take a hit. You said everything tastes good when you're with Lloyd, right?" Riho's eyes were like steel.

She was really holding this fake date against Selen.

"Wait...a 'hit'? That's not a word that applies to soup!"

"Selen," Marie said, her voice like velvet, "I made this just for you. Witch's soup."

"Your eyes aren't matching your tone!"

"Drop dead!"

Childish grandmas did not mince words.

"Hey, Alka! Be subtle! Sweeten the pot!" warned Riho.

"How sweet it is doesn't matter. It'll still dissolve her stomach lining and spread the poison to the rest of her organs! Who cares about taste?"

"Marie, it's Alka's delivery that Riho wanted sweetened— Wait, poison? Did you say poison?"

Riho grabbed Selen's shoulder and held a spoon to her lips.

"Ha! Blame Mena for not stopping your rampage… Mm? Where *is* Mena?"

A moment ago, she'd been on the verge of a starvation-fueled temper tantrum, but there was no sign of her now.

Then, in the distance, they heard her strangled shriek.

"Phyllo! Not that way!"

Mena came rushing past, trailing an expressionless drunk. Both headed right for the kitchen.

"…I want grape juice."

"That was wine! You've gotta be grown up to drink that! No, don't… Phyllo!"

Mena was definitely full-on desperate—and Phyllo did actually stop.

"…I have to be grown up… Then I'll have my master make a woman out of me!"

"That's not the qualifying factor! Lloyd, run! Phyllo's still drunk! She'll steal you first!"

But this warning only alerted Phyllo to Lloyd's presence.

"…There you are."

With no lead-up at all, Phyllo vaulted in their direction with physical abilities rivaling those of anyone from Kunlun. Lloyd moved too late, and she caught him.

"Ah!"

Phyllo straddled Lloyd, staring down at him, expressionless.

"……I'm gonna puke," she said. From her current angle, that would mean a critical hit on Lloyd's face.

"Wait! This is a restaurant!" Riho shouted, somehow clinging to the memory of being employed here. She tried rubbing Phyllo's back.

"It'll be a lifelong trauma for the both of you!" Marie said, speaking from personal experience. This made her very convincing. "You'll let out a weird shriek every time you remember!"

"Yes! Allow me to mount him in your place!"

Half-grown grandmas have no concept of restraint. Alka was definitely the type to floor it, no matter what street she was driving down.

"Right. Have some soup and calm down," Selen offered, trying to deftly rid herself of the tainted dish.

With everyone acting at odds, the scene was total chaos. And they were attracting considerable attention.

"Don't drink that, Phyllo! It might well stop your heart."

"You served me something dangerous enough to stop my *heart*?!" Selen shrieked.

"......Urp."

"Calm down, everyone! Something dangerous might come out of Phyllo!"

"Calm down and switch places with me, Phyllo," urged Alka.

"Please be quiet!"

A sudden roar from Lloyd, of all people. Everyone froze, looking at him.

Lloyd put Phyllo on his chair, gently rubbing her back.

"There's a lot to say here, but...Chief, Marie?"

""Uh...yes?"" they squeaked, like students yelled at by the teacher who never rose their voice at anyone.

Giving them a stern look, Lloyd said, "I asked you *not* to come here."

""Uh...right...""

"I know you must be worried about me, but I can't have you showing up at work all the time."

The main point of concern should have been their motivation—crossing half the continent just to see Lloyd dressed as a bellboy.

But for Lloyd, it was like his having his parents show up only to make a scene... Naturally, even he got mad.

"Crap, Marie! Lloyd's mad at us!" Alka yelped.

Marie nodded. "Yes… Switch to Plan B."

She adjusted her glasses, putting the alternate plan into action. "That's not why we're here, Lloyd. Have you forgotten what I do in the shadows?"

Lloyd thought for a second, and then realization dawned.

"Y-you mean…"

Marie nodded. Lloyd was convinced she was the secret hero saving Azami, though it was actually Lloyd who'd saved the realm… He just hadn't realized it.

"Yes. Fact is, there's a plot being hatched somewhere nearby that could upend the entire kingdom," Marie said, rattling off her prepared excuse. "I've asked Chief Alka to assist me in investigating. By pure, bizarre coincidence, we happen to be where you're working."

Everyone was listening. This seemed to be going a little *too* well. Marie was getting worried, but she stuck to her guns.

"I've got a pretty good idea who's behind all this, so I figured no time like the present. That's why I came rushing here."

"Yes! We're absolutely not here to gawk at you in your bellboy uniform, Lloyd!"

Marie tried to stop Alka from blurting out anything else.

"So you know who's putting everyone in comas?!" Lloyd exclaimed, gazing at her with respect.

"Yes, I know it's hard to believe," Marie continued. "Uh…comas?"

This was news to her. Baffled, she looked at the others…who grimly returned her gaze.

"I see… So the realm's taking this seriously enough for you to get personally involved," Riho started.

"Huh?"

"I just assumed you were here to see Sir Lloyd. I apologize," added Selen.

"Huh?"

"The realm only ordered a formal investigation yesterday… Just who are you, witch?" asked Mena.

"Huh?"

"......Mm," offered Phyllo.

"Mm?"

Marie was getting more lost by the second.

"Marie," Alka whispered, "I think there's actually something going on here."

"A hotel incident? Like in a mystery novel?!"

And Marie had just cast herself in the role of the detective about to reveal whodunnit.

As realization dawned, her confident smile faded. This was the climax of the novel, the moment when the culprit was identified.

"Marie, you're in trouble! Maybe better to admit you're lying? Lloyd probably won't talk to you for a week, but nothing worse, at least."

"A week? I don't know if I'd survive that..."

"Don't be silly! Go on, be honest, yell 'Gotcha!' with a big smile..."

"Master, this is serious."

Why was this happening to her? Marie frowned, trying to find a way out.

"Oh? This all sounds very intriguing." Threonine had broken off his conversation with Selen's father and was striding toward them. "You know who's behind the comas?"

"Lord Threonine, pay no attention to the babblings of these suspicious individuals," his secretary protested.

Threonine ignored him, fixing Marie with a pointed glare.

Cowed, Marie took a step back. "Uh, why are you so interested?"

He was a total stranger to her, but from the look of him, she knew that if she yelled "Gotcha," he'd probably sock her in the face and send her teeth flying everywhere.

But then, Coba ran over with a bucket (having reacted swiftly to the word *puke*), ready to catch anything that came out of Phyllo. He seemed relieved to see her looking better, but then saw trouble brewing between a witch and a local lord and reassumed his worried expression.

"Uh...Lord Threonine and...young lady...what's going on here?"

There was quite a crowd watching. He needed to contain the situation.

Threonine glanced at Coba and at Selen's father, who had started following him over, and scowled.

"Well, well...what fortuitous timing. It seems this witch has figured out who's behind the string of incidents involving the unconscious victims."

He sounded like he thought all the suspects had arrived.

"The culprit? Hmm..." Since Coba's prime suspect was Threonine, he read something else into that—and began looking suspiciously from Threonine to Marie.

And since Threonine's prime suspect was Coba, he took Coba's reaction as an obvious performance.

"What's all the fuss about?" Selen's father demanded, joining them.

Threonine decided to close the case. "You've heard the stories about people turning up in comas? Seems this black-robed detective knows who's responsible. You might want to hear this."

"Really?" Selen's father said, baffled.

"Really?" Marie repeated, but this was a horrified response to being called a detective.

Coba was studying her behavior, as well as her garb. His frown deepened.

"You're clearly not law enforcement...so just who are you? If you're putting on an act in the hopes of a payout, I suggest you leave."

"Er, no, nothing like *that*...," Marie said with absolutely no follow-up. Which was natural, seeing as she'd only just heard about the trouble and had been lying through her teeth.

Threonine appeared skeptical, too.

"Do you really know who's doing it? You'd better not be lying for money. Not after getting my hopes up."

This potential betrayal had his stony visage looking even craggier.

"Eep," Marie shrieked. This was clearly life or death.

"Hold on a minute!" Lloyd interjected, stepping in. "I can vouch for Marie. She's not the sort of person who'd lie about this. She solves cases from the shadows all the time!"

"Uh-huh..."

This was less help than a bullet in the back. Lloyd's well-intentioned attempt to vouch for her had made it even harder to backpedal.

"Really…?"

But of course, no one would believe a claim like Lloyd's without evidence. Marie still had a chance of insisting she was just Lloyd's roommate—but then she saw how the two men reacted.

"Well, if Lloyd says so, it *must* be true!"

"I see. You're a friend of Lloyd's! Then your deductions *must* be sound!"

All suspicion had melted away completely. In fact, every staff member in the vicinity was nodding happily.

"Why does everyone have such absolute faith in Lloyd?"

"I know just how you feel, Marie," Riho sympathized, clapping her on the back.

But now Marie had to deal with two older men gazing at her expectantly. And all of Lloyd's friends. Escape was no longer an option.

Alka leaned in and whispered, "Marie, you've got to buy some time."

"Stall? Right…"

She desperately tried to smooth things over.

"Um, so…b-basically, Alka and I have already nipped things in the bud. Don't worry."

This was "basically" a lie. Given that Alka looked like a little girl, her corroboration wasn't particularly convincing. But…

"Oh! I see Lloyd was right to place his trust in you. You've already eliminated the monsters!"

Their faith in Lloyd was enough to make any old crap sound meaningful.

"…Monsters?"

A stir ran through the crowd.

"I-I'll go call the police!" Threonine's secretary yelped, dashing into the hall.

The word *police* proved to be the final nail in the coffin, and the situation was now permanently out of control. The crowd had been watching like some sort of dinner theater, but now they were beginning to look genuinely alarmed.

Marie certainly was. She pulled Alka into a corner, pleading for advice.

"Master! I took your advice, but I think it made things worse!" she whispered.

Alka grinned maliciously. "Well, then I'll just have to go investigate—starting in the hot springs! You buy me more time!"

"You tricked me! Now there's no way out!"

Marie finally realized Alka had been setting her up. She took a step toward the underdeveloped grandma, her blood boiling.

A mini vaudeville act was unfolding in the corner of the restaurant. Riho and Selen had seen this before and realized at once what was really going on.

"I didn't trick anybody! Don't you worry! I'll just wait till you're entirely at the end of your rope, covered in cold sweat, and collapsed from panic, and then I'll use an ancient rune to wipe everyone's memories for you," Alka whispered.

This dreadful solution only made Marie angrier.

"You can't do that! Think of something now! This instant!"

"You should never have turned me into your horse," Alka said smugly. "Let's hit this hot spring! Work up a sweat in the sauna! Come, Lloyd, we'll just get in the way of Marie's detective work! I fancy a soak. Everyone can join us!"

"Er...but...the culprit?" Lloyd hesitated, radiating pure faith in Marie.

Riho clapped him on the shoulder. "Come on."

"Master! You're abandoning me?! I want to use the hot springs, too!" Marie cried.

"And you will! Once you're absolutely drenched in flop sweat. Good luck!"

"You little hag!"

But Marie's agonized shriek was powerless before the lure of the hot springs.

"So who's responsible for these attacks?" Threonine growled.

Utterly abandoned, Marie only had one option...

"Well, let's not rush, here. First, we'll have to review the facts of the case. Let's see... What was the first incident?"

"...You don't know? Can we really trust this girl?" Selen's father asked. A legitimate question.

"Of course we can! Lloyd guaranteed it!" Threonine bellowed.

"Absolutely. Our hotel has placed its faith in Lloyd—his word is all we need," Coba chimed in.

Selen's father did not look satisfied, but ignoring him, Marie threw herself into this strategy.

"R-right, we need to view the situation as a whole! I'm aware of all the particulars, of course! Thoroughly aware."

"Very well... Let's begin with the first incident that occurred here in the hotel, all so we can expose the culprit."

"Mm, let's catch this villain!"

Coba and Threonine locked eyes, smiling broadly. Everyone could almost see the angry puffs of smoke between them.

"........."

Meanwhile, Selen's father just gave Marie a suspicious glare. The crowd around them seemed equally dubious.

"...That's understandable, yeah. How did Lloyd get these two to trust him so completely? Anyway, gotta keep up the detective act... Damn that kid grandma..."

Marie was forced to maintain her pretense while she awaited Alka's return.

"I knew it! I knew she was making it all up! Argh!" Riho howled, her voice echoing off the stones of the bath.

Without the ribbon in her hair, Riho seemed like a totally different person—aside from her mechanical arm and decidedly middle-aged mannerisms. She dunked her face underwater and made bubbles.

"Yeah. Sorry. I never imagined there was *actually* something happening here," Alka admitted, stepping into the bath behind Riho. Her smooth skin and flat chest were adolescent, while her satisfied groan betrayed her grandma nature.

"Well, if we wrap this thing up too fast, I'll have to head back, so… let's take our time soaking!" Mena was the first to sound her actual age. "And there's nothing like post-bath ale!"

Consider that earlier statement redacted: They were *all* acting like old-timers.

"So what are *you* doing, m'lady?"

"I've never been in a hot spring before!" said Selen, hovering nervously around the edge.

"Just get in already! C'mon!" Riho grabbed her arm and yanked.

"Hot! Yow! Don't do that!"

Selen's porcelain skin instantly flushed red. Riho burst out laughing.

"Bwa-ha-ha! Normally, I can't get past your cursed belt, but now it's payback time!"

"Riho! Hot springs are no place for pranks!"

"It's only us here, so who cares? I can do *whatever* I want!" Mena said, sneaking up behind Selen with a broad grin and grabbing her boobs.

"Whoa! Mena! Hey!"

"Grr… Th-that's it!"

Turning bright red, Selen wheeled around and went to get even, hands flexing.

Ladies and gentlemen, your contestants:

Riho, the slender one!

Mena, the petite one!

And Alka, the little hag!

Wordlessly, Selen lowered her hands again, looking very sorry for them.

"Your silence hurts the worst!"

Silence could sometimes lead to injury. Of the heart.

"Right, right!" Alka, meanwhile, had started swimming around. First, freestyle, then butterfly, then sidestroke. She was as unrestrained in the bath as she was in life. Kid grandmas exist in the Venn diagram between little girl and ancient crone, beings with no redeeming features.

"...If it's only us here, all rules cease to exist. Very educational," Selen muttered.

Riho looked around. "What happened to Phyllo?"

"Sweating in the sauna... The grape juice is almost outta her system, but when she saw the water pouring out of that lion head, she almost puked again."

They'd been seconds from having the alkaline hot springs spiked with stomach acid.

Alka clearly had questions about Phyllo. "That girl... She's a very skilled fighter."

"You noticed, kid?"

"Yes, there's an old man in our village who moves the same way."

"Really? Not many like that...maybe they're from the same style? Phyllo's was started by a warrior they called the Fierce God..."

"Yeah, Pyrid used to be a real troublemaker! Went around telling everyone to call him by that silly name."

Mena looked confused, so Alka introduced herself properly.

"Name's Alka, chief of Kunlun. You've heard of it? In legends?"

"...What?"

"This sure is a nice bath! I reckon I feel ten years younger. Of course, once you pass a hundred, ten years don't make much difference..."

The one-two punch of a legendary village and Alka's actual age left Mena reeling.

But...she'd seen firsthand what Lloyd could do, which left her unable to dismiss the notion. It actually kind of explained a lot. Explained everything, really. Still stunned, she turned to Riho and Selen for answers.

"......Is this true?"

"You're better off forgetting."

"Knowledge leads to ruin."

What great advice.

"Come on, Mena... Adapting to any situation is half of being a grown-up... Okay, I've adapted!"

Hot springs were supposed to be relaxing, but Mena felt quite the opposite. She sank into the water, blowing bubbles. Putting things out of one's mind was a vital skill.

"......And I'm back," Phyllo intoned, steam rising off her body as she emerged from the sauna hiding absolutely nothing, totally exposed—except for the steam covering all the convenient places.

"Right, since everyone's here, can I get a rundown of what's going on?" Alka plunked herself on the edge of the bath, getting the ball rolling.

"Well, basically..." Riho brought her up to speed.

"......I had no idea," Phyllo said, gravely soaking herself.

"Phyllo...," Selen said. "You're here because Azami ordered you to investigate all this."

"......I may be missing some memories... I think more grape juice might help me remember..."

Mena and Riho desperately begged her to stop, while Alka slid into the water, grinning maliciously.

"I see," she muttered. "So treants are behind this... Marie must be in deep by now."

Riho caught the word *treant*. "I knew it! It is treants, then?"

"From what I've heard. Not fatal, but three days and nights in a coma... Nothing grabs passing travelers and animals and sucks the life out of them like a darn treant."

Mena came swimming over, dog-paddling like a child, even though she was in her twenties!

"Hang on—Allan collapsed in the bath. Is there a treant growing inside the hotel?"

"No. I reckon the sapling has infected someone like a parasite. It can control its host, grow its power, and find a good spot to put down roots and stake out a territory."

"So someone *is* infected... That's always nasty. If we mess this up, the casualties will be so huge, they'll have to redraw maps."

Mena sighed into the bathwater, regretting having accepted the job.

"Don't worry, Mena! Fate brought me. I'll help you wrap this up."

Riho shot her a suspicious look. It wasn't like Alka to be *helpful*.

"Marie said it was forbidden for villagers from Kunlun to run around helping people. You're sure?"

"I've never liked standing by when people are in trouble. And with Lloyd's friend Allan dead, I've got to act."

"He didn't *actually* die…"

Alka blew right past that, walking naked over to the windows and staring out.

"Well, we need to investigate the scene. Let's all head to the suite's outdoor bath! I reckon Lloyd's probably there."

"That's your real goal!" Riho's cries echoed through the room.

"No, no, they say killers always return to the scene of the crime. It's our best option!"

"You're definitely doing this for the wrong reasons! Also, put some clothes on."

"What idiot gets dressed moments before offering to wash a boy's back?! This way!"

She was *clearly* only in this for the chance to take a bath with him. Riho clutched her head, but Selen went right past her.

"Thoroughly inspecting the scene of the crime is basic police work!" she said.

"You'll end up getting arrested!"

"…………"

"Refusing to reply doesn't make peeping legal!"

Mena started giggling. "You don't seem to be trying *that* hard to stop them."

"Wha— Mena?!"

That hit close to home. Well, everyone wanted to bathe with their crush.

"Look, everyone's going to Lloyd's bath!"

"You all suck. If Marie finds out you spied on Lloyd bathing, she'll… dislocate her jaw, probably."

Shaking her head as if she'd been forced into going along with them, Riho made her way outside, toward the bath where Allan had passed out.

Detective in a Pickle: Suppose You Gathered Suspects Without Getting Briefed on the Crime Itself

Meanwhile, the fake detective Marie was listening to Coba's rundown of the facts while desperately trying to find a way out of this mess.

What should I do? She said to buy time, but we're talking Alka. She'll never come back. She's forgotten all about who's behind this. She's just enjoying the hot springs while I get wrung out like an old rag… Argh, I *want a bath!* I *want to wash Lloyd's back!*

Not the most focused chain of thoughts, but hey, it was all part of her charm.

"At first, we thought it was an isolated incident, but over the last few months, the number of victims has risen sharply… Are you listening, Detective?"

"…Uh, you mean me? I'm listening!" Marie squeaked.

She'd seemed a little out of it, which made Coba worry.

Right, I have to learn the facts here. I don't even know what I'm dealing with… Maybe my trained gray matter will actually be able to crack the case!

Her mind made up, Marie listened closely.

"A number of victims from the hotel staff and neighboring residents…"

"Oh?"

Occasionally confused by Marie's surprised responses to the available information, Coba finished his explanation.

"Those are all the facts I'm aware of related to these incidents."

"Hmm."

"Which is why we're so flummoxed by it all… Detective?"

Marie was staring into space, frowning, her mouth pursed. Coba leaned in, looking concerned.

Aha! I have no clue.

On the inside, Marie had already given up on finding the culprit. Perhaps it was not her brain cells but her mental discipline that needed honing.

No. There's no way I could possibly solve this case! But I can hardly admit I was lying now!

She had to find a way to get out of this while preserving her role as a detective. There was only one thing she could think of...

Right! The hapless detectives in mystery novels! I've just gotta spout crap like they do! It's like when they try their best, but it still doesn't work out. Poor loveable, hapless detective! They might be disappointed by this new performance, but it's better than getting caught lying!

Marie decided the best way out of this was to come up with a deliberately ridiculous solution. In mystery novels and manga, detectives who give wrong answers don't get yelled at much. Everyone just shakes their heads.

Maybe, Marie thought, *it's actually a good idea.*

Her plan clear, Marie started psyching herself up.

No time like the present! Just act nothing like myself, and I'll be fine!

It was more like her usual self, but...well, consider this part of her charm, too. Or her haplessness.

Her expression went from serious to disappointed to filled with hope.

"Uh, are you really doing okay?" Threonine said. "I mean, if Lloyd trusts you, I'm sure we can, but..."

"Yes," Marie said. Imagine a crash zoom to her face. "I have seen the path I need to take."

Her cryptic declaration drew dubious looks from everyone, but Marie was way past caring. She began prattling nonsense while looking extremely proud of herself.

"From what I've heard, there are no signs of any humans or weapons around, so you believed it to be the work of a monster...but that's what the culprit *wanted* you to think. It was all a scheme to avoid suspicion."

"Oh-ho! But how would one go about draining the life out of someone without leaving any trace behind?"

Threonine's argument made perfect sense, but Marie's manner remained confident. Someone improvising for her life was not so easily dissuaded. Marie just carried on rattling out the first thing that popped into her head, heedless of how ridiculous it sounded.

"They jumped! Using powers far beyond that of your ordinary human, they leaped from treetop to treetop, scrambled up the hotel walls and back to their room, leaving no trace behind, then carried on as if nothing was out of the ordinary. It's elementary, really."

Complete crap.

Marie was fully expecting everyone to go, "What's elementary about it?" Or maybe even, "So it *is* a monster!" She looked to see how Threonine and Coba were taking this.

But their reactions…

"Well, if you know that much, you're very good indeed, Detective."

"Hmm…I did have my doubts, but I can see why Lloyd vouched for you. Sorry for testing you."

They seemed very convinced. Marie had not seen that coming.

Whaaaat? Why are they acting impressed? What the hell is *this case?!*

They were both clearly looking at her expectantly. Marie was forced to pile on the lies, hoping to get herself back on the hapless track.

"Uh, um…so, well, anyone could guess *that.* Even an amateur!"

"No need for modesty, Detective. A brilliant deduction proves both your knowledge and the extent of your investigation."

Marie was starting to realize she might be in *real* trouble here. She had to add more crappy deductions before she drowned in the swamp.

"…That's when I realized the culprit's real motive!"

"Real motive? What?"

They were hanging on her every word.

"Namely: world conquest!"

""World conquest?!"" Coba and Threonine harmonized.

"Yes… They're using the stolen life power to create minions and spread their power across the continent. The culprit will become a demon lord, an enemy of mankind…I think!"

Marie wrapped things up, her deductions—or ramblings—somehow drawing to a close.

If I say something that absurd, nobody will believe me! They'll think I've got mental problems and decide they want nothing to do with me! They'll take back what they just said! They'll send me to see a good psychiatrist and throw me out!

Marie prepared herself to be evicted, leaning forward, ready for someone to angrily grab a fistful of her robe.

But these efforts proved in vain, as Threonine and Coba both said: ""Makes sense!""

In harmony again! Had they met under different circumstances, these two might well have become best friends.

Whaaaaat? Howww? Whyyyyyyyy?!

Marie's eyes were ready to pop out of her head. But neither man noticed. They both folded their arms, groaning.

"Yes...right here on the road connecting Rokujou to Azami. If they increase their numbers..."

"...Using the illegal cultivation to fund their army while waiting for their chance to strike... It doesn't take much thought to see how that would work. This is how they were preparing their invasion..."

A terrifying torrent of words was pouring out of them, and Marie's eye was starting to twitch.

What's going on here is so much worse than I imagined! This isn't a case for a detective at all! Call in the damn army!

She didn't need honed brain cells or mental fortitude. She needed an exorcism—a legitimate one.

Of course, the two of them both knew that treants were behind all this, so they'd found her words very convincing. As nobody else knew that simple fact, though, the crowd still looked very dubious.

Realizing this, Coba attempted to explain.

"Actually...and please don't be alarmed..."

He explained the illegal treant cultivation, that someone infected with the seedling was among them, and that this person's physical powers were greatly enhanced.

""""What?!"""" Guests and staff alike were horrified. So was Marie.

"...Why were *you* surprised?"

"Er, uh...just going with the flow?" Marie suggested, a cold sweat forming on her brow.

Wait! You have to tell me these things! Illegal treant cultivation? I can't play a hapless detective if I accidentally get it right!

These unexpected developments had Marie at her wits' end.

Coba was doing his best to calm the assembled guests.

"We've kept this under wraps to avoid inciting undue concern..."

But if there was someone infected by a treant close by...... The guests and staff were all starting to eye one other suspiciously.

Any minute now, someone would say, "I won't be in the same room as a monster! I'm going back to my room!" That would ensure their own doom.

The restaurant was abuzz.

Seizing his chance, Threonine's voice echoed through the dining hall.

"But fear not! This detective has already identified the culprit! They'll drag this villain out into the light of day! Where the iron fist of justice can pulverize them!"

His booming voice echoed in the pit of their stomachs, and the crowd visibly relaxed, sighing with relief.

Marie did the opposite, drawing a quick, panicked breath, her heart beating a mile a minute, her chest swaying from the sudden expansion.

He raised the stakes! And I've got no escape!

This was a crisis. Her plan to worm her way out with trumped-up nonsense had backfired completely, and now she was teetering on the edge of a cliff.

Coba approached her, frowning. He was convinced Threonine was the criminal and the whole speech about iron fists was just an attempt to confuse the issue.

"Detective, I think it's high time you got down to business. Who is this villain? Who must be crushed beneath the fist of justice?"

That's what I wanna know!

"Mm, it's about time we learned the truth. Lay it on us, Detective," Threonine pressured, moving closer to Coba, eyes like daggers. They gave the impression of two boxers before a match.

Stuck between them like their referee, Marie was totally lost. She had no way of knowing each was convinced the other was the culprit.

"Who did this, Detective?!"

"End this farce! Make your accusation!"

She gulped nervously.

"Uh, the culprit is..."

""Yes?!""

Marie just stopped caring at all.

I don't know the dumb answer! I'm just gonna point at someone at random and insist they did it! The little hag said she could reset everyone's memories later, right?!

She pushed the scowling men out of the way, pointing at nothing in particular.

"The villain behind these assaults...is you! Probably."

All eyes followed her finger. And the unfortunate victim standing there...

"Me?"

It was Selen's father. Despite the sudden accusation, he was staring back at Marie, completely calm.

"I see... I've been putting people in comas, have I?"

His voice was so quiet, Marie was already getting ready to prostrate herself before him, apologizing profusely for her error.

But before she could, Threonine raised his voice.

"That was a blind spot...the master of the Hemein family. He's certainly in a position to head up the illegal cultivation! I was convinced it was the owner here, but..."

"You were? And here I thought it was you, Lord Threonine."

Having convinced themselves of the real culprit, they advanced on Selen's father.

Finding himself cornered, the man frowned. "My family involved in illegal cultivation...for world conquest?"

He adjusted his collar, calmly facing everyone.

His confidence just seemed to make Threonine angry.

"Yeah, your family's been spreading their wings lately—on the profits from treant wood!"

"Yes, we have been doing well for ourselves—but trading in treant lumber itself is *not* illegal, as I'm sure you're well aware."

"Hngg, and here I thought Coba did it," Threonine raged. "But you framed him while cultivating and selling it yourself!"

"Um, if we could just calm down and discuss this rationally?"

Threonine wasn't listening. He began aggressively interrogating Selen's father.

"That's not all! Why arrange a marriage with my idiot son *now*? Were you hoping to rope the Lidocaines into helping you spread the treants, using our knowledge of the area? Start explaining! Leave nothing out!"

Threonine's meaty hand had grabbed the front of Selen's father's shirt. They were both local lords, but one was a soldier and the other a businessman. The physical difference was considerable.

But Selen's father remained undaunted.

"You are sorely lacking in rationality, Threonine."

"I'm *what*—gah!"

Selen's father had grabbed Threonine's wrist.

"Hngg...gggh!"

Threonine was turning bright red, struggling—while Selen's father showed no signs of anything at all. Threonine was forced to release him.

Threonine's wrist had turned somewhat purple. He, Coba, and the crowd were clearly rattled; Selen's father did not give the impression of having that kind of strength.

"How are you so strong? What have you—?"

"It's no big deal," Selen's father said, as if nothing out of the ordinary had occurred. He took a seat on a nearby chair. "Now, let us all discuss this like civilized men. I have plenty of questions myself. Detective, will you grant me a little time?"

"Er...yeah, sure," Marie stammered, surprised to be dragged back into this.

Selen's father began speaking.

"About the rumors of illegal treant cultivation…"

A little earlier, the "idiot son" had made his way to the kitchen.

"Passed out in the sauna and waking up in nothing but a bathrobe," Allan muttered. "Throat parched, *and* I'm starving… This is awful."

There seemed to be some sort of fight going on in the restaurant where the doors were closed, so Allan had gone to the kitchen instead, hoping to at least snag a bread roll. But…

"Th-there's no one here?"

Alone in the kitchen in his bathrobe, Allan had been hoping he could promise to pay later…and then spied a steaming pot on the stove. Gulping, he took a look inside. There was soup in the pot—no promising chunks of any kind but a strong herbal aroma wafted up from the concoction.

"…I'm really sorry. I can't wait," he said to no one in particular. He picked up a nearby ladle. "You can tell this is a first-class-hotel soup! Looks simple, but that scent has *layers*."

Allan quickly took a sip, like the owner of a ramen shop taste-testing his wares. He had that kind of expression.

Gulp, gulp, gulp—Allan was so thirsty, he started chugging the soup like a post-workout sports drink.

"Richly flavored—really grows on 'oo, I fink…"

One sip of that balm could numb the mouth, and Allan had downed enough to spread the effect through his entire body. He collapsed on the spot.

As his consciousness faded, Allan swore he'd file a complaint with whoever made the dish later.

The only sound left in the kitchen was the forlorn bubbling from the soup pot.

Meanwhile, Lloyd was in the outdoor bath. This was a hot spring set aside for suite guests only, so no one else was around. He felt a little uncomfortable enjoying such a luxurious facility just because he had taken Allan's place.

"Should I really be relaxing? Especially given how hard Riho's been working..."

He was here to work but had been thrust into a role that had somehow led to him enjoying a hot spring. Naturally, he felt guilty about that.

"I'm lying to a lot of people... I should at least find out who's behind these coma incidents and make everyone feel safe. Hmm?"

Lloyd suddenly felt eyes on him from outside. He moved over to the window, staring out into the darkness.

"I feel like someone's watching me...or is it my imagination?"

Deciding to get back in the water, he peeled off the towel at his waist and turned around.

"Yoo-hoo! How's it going, buddy?"

Alka, the kid-sized grandma, burst in, brushing through the curtains like a boisterous regular, naked as the day she was born, her childlike body on full display.

Unfortunately, Lloyd had been caught just between removing his towel and resubmerging in the steamy bathwater.

"..........." (Lloyd was flustered.)

"..........." (Alka's eyes locked downstairs.)

"..............Ah." (Lloyd turned red.)

"..............*Psshht!*" (Alka sprayed blood from her nose.)

All in 0.5 seconds.

Lloyd had his crotch covered in a fraction of a second, but Alka's superhuman reflexes activated, allowing her eyes to catch a clear glimpse of his nether regions.

With a look of ecstasy, Alka twirled her nude body, spraying nose blood all over the bathroom floor.

The rest of the girls came running in a moment later. Some had managed to wrap themselves in bath towels, some had not—all were definitely naked.

"Wha— Why are you all here?!" Lloyd shrieked.

"Th-there's a good reason, Lloyd!" Riho yelped, making sure the towel around her was tight. She was bright red. "Chief Alka said she wanted to check out the suite bath—"

But Selen burst past her, moving like the wind, eyes like hearts.

"Sir Lloyd! The two of us are basically family! Bathing together like family is only natural! You can do whatever you like in a hot spring as long as it's only us here!"

This was clearly a problem, but so was Phyllo's total lack of effort to cover any of her ridiculously taut martial artist's body.

"...Master and student are also like family...and we will someday marry..."

Bringing up the rear was Mena, sailing in with complete aplomb, holding a single washcloth vertically so it just barely covered upstairs and downstairs. That had to be *somebody's* fetish.

"So why is Chief Alka knocked out? Did she slip and fall?" Mena asked.

Lloyd turned bright red again. "......Eep."

Selen pounced on *that* response. "Did you just *squeak*, Lloyd? You can't mean—"

Riho's eyes narrowed. "She...saw you, Lloyd?"

Super-embarrassed, Lloyd nodded.

"......Let's just bury her," Phyllo suggested, grabbing Alka by the scruff of her neck.

"Why does Alka have all the luck?! It's not fair! Sir Lloyd! I demand you show me, too!"

"Hang on! There's no fair or unfair when it comes to nudity!"

"Don't worry! I'll make it fair! You can look at me naked all you like! Touch me if you—"

Riho was about to further debate the semantics of *fair*, but first...

"......Mm?" Phyllo suddenly stared into the distance, as if she'd noticed something.

"What's up, Phyllo?" Mena said, concerned.

"...There." Phyllo suddenly hurled Alka out the window.

Rustle, rustle! Snap! Srack... Foosh. Flap, flap, flap. Caw, caw.

Alka went crashing through the trees and slid across the ground, and then the forest's silence was filled with flapping wings and bird cries.

"Phyllo, I sympathize, but if you're gonna throw someone naked from this height, you should really tie a rope to them first," Selen scolded.

She sympathized a little too much…

Riho and Selen both chastised Phyllo, but it was pretty clear she was preventing them from torturing Alka themselves.

"You threw her pretty dang far, Phyllo… Why?" Mena asked, not once taking her eyes off the direction of Alka's descent.

"…They ran."

"Huh? Who did?"

"…Whoever was watching."

"Er… This is a family bath. Most peeping toms are going to be after the women's room."

"Chief Alka and Selen are the biggest peepers, and since they're here with us, that means… Well, one is dearly departed, I guess." Riho crossed herself to pay her respects.

Alka isn't dead, though.

"Invading the bath is actually worse than peeping… Who's trying to peep on Lloyd?"

"Marie's busy now," Selen muttered gravely. "Could it be…Allan?"

Yeah, no. He had been knocked out again.

The actual peeper was Kikyou, who'd been watching Lloyd in the bath through binoculars.

Of course, unlike *some* people (read: Selen and Alka), she was not motivated by carnal desire.

Convinced Lloyd was infected by a treant sapling, she had determined that the only way to find out where it was attached to him was to stake out the bath, where he was most likely to disrobe.

"My plot to put the balm in the soup, administering it orally and flushing out the seedling, failed… And the lie I had to use to get the chefs out of there was really forced… But who were those girls?"

While she'd been making the soup, Alka and Marie had burst in and intoned, *"LEAVE!"* in a death growl, their faces twisted in rictuses of horror—symptoms of their Lloyd deprivation. Kikyou's decision to flee the scene had definitely been a wise one.

"Argh, and I left the balm behind… I'll have to fetch it later— There!"

Her binoculars had finally caught Lloyd nude.

"Doesn't seem like the balm is working at all… I guess I had to smear it exactly where the sapling is… Ugh, with the light stones reflecting, I can't see anything—the steam's in the way, too…"

The seedling must have been attached to his crotch, and Kikyou strained her eyes trying to get a good glimpse of it, following his every move.

"Oh, he's a good boy. Washing up before he enters the bath… All I can see is his back… Oh! Argh, he's in the water now. So close!" she shrieked, getting worked up.

What am I even doing?

Part of her was shaking her head at the mess in which she found herself, objectively observing her actions.

Instead of doing this, I could just tell him the truth… Worse comes to worst, I'd end up killing him, but…

If the seedling matured, hordes of people would die. The life of one boy was a small price to pay.

I wish I could think like that.

"My dream's come true at last!"

……Dammit.

Lloyd's bright smile kept echoing through Kikyou's mind.

"If your dream's come true, then protect yourself!" she grumbled, clutching her head. Then she focused her attention on the bath again.

But what was going on now? She'd taken her eyes off it for a second, and the place was swarming with girls!

"Wait, do I have the wrong bath?"

But Lloyd was still in there, so it had to be the right place… Kikyou squinted, watching the scene carefully.

No one was getting in the water. They were all just standing and talking.

"What are they doing?" Kikyou wondered.

She was still puzzled when one of the women suddenly looked right at her.

"Huh? Did she see me? At *this* distance?"

Then something white came hurtling right toward her.

"What? Oh, crap!"

Kikyou scrambled to avoid the flying object and lost her balance, falling out of the tree.

"Oww… What? That looked human…"

Then a figure appeared from the forest. Had they heard the noise and come to look?

"…Who's there?"

Anyone coming from the depths of the forest had to be—

"Erm. Oh? What are you doing here? You're hotel staff, right?"

It was Threonine's secretary. He was looking at Kikyou with surprise and seemed somewhat nervous. His clothes had leaves and twigs stuck to them, like he'd been following an animal around…not what you'd call an evening stroll.

"What are *you* doing? It's dangerous to walk outdoors at night." Kikyou pretended as if she didn't know who he was—to disguise her own connection to Threonine.

"It doesn't make sense for me to be here, does it? I'm aware of that. Damn that witch… She was lying about having taken care of things! I had to hurry and check, but everything was fine!"

What was he talking about? Frowning, she leaned in for a better look.

"Are you hiding something?" she asked, taking a wild stab in the dark.

This rattled the secretary far more than she'd expected.

"I-I'm not hiding anything! This is just a perfectly ordinary cypress!"

"A cypress? You hid something in that tree? Step aside!"

She pushed him back, checking the trunk. There was a hollow inside it and a really twisted tree stuffed into the opening.

"I-is this…?"

"The illegally cultivated treant."

The secretary's tone had changed completely.

Kikyou gasped.

All trace of fluster had vanished—as if he knew he'd been caught red-handed, so there was no point keeping up the act.

"You're aware of the treant?" he asked.

"Y-yes…I've heard…rumors…"

Why was he asking her? The secretary just chuckled.

"Don't bother. I know exactly who you are. The odd-jobs girl Threonine hired. Kikyou."

She went tense, pulling a knife from her pocket.

But the secretary didn't move. It was as if all emotion had drained from him.

"Don't worry. I'm only telling you this because I wish to make a deal."

"A deal?"

His eyes gleamed behind his glasses. "I know how much Threonine is paying you. I'll double it."

"Well…that's certainly underhanded."

As if he'd expected her to say that, the secretary took a document out of his pocket.

"Details of the transactions, making Threonine out to be the dealer. I'd appreciate it if you could give this to the police and leave me out of it."

"You're certainly prepared. So has your goal always been to drag Threonine down? He *was* pretty mean to you…"

This seemed to touch a nerve. All his pent-up frustrations with his employer erupted out of him.

"'Mean' barely covers it! That man was a warrior. He favors anyone strong over anyone with actual business skills, and we suffer for it! Even after promoting me to secretary, he doesn't treat me any differently! So I started cultivating treants! I'm going to turn his beloved mountains into a treant horde and make his rivals, the Hemeins, rich in the process! Then I'll pin the whole thing on him, while myself becoming a being no one can touch—!"

This was getting more and more disturbing, with the latter bits sounding downright supernatural.

"Wh-what do you mean by that?"

The secretary twitched. Then he was eerily calm again, as if the fit had never happened at all.

"You feel obligated to turn me down? Missing this opportunity will be your loss, odd-jobs girl."

He seemed confident she would take the document. His eyes said so.

Kikyou felt no anger. Her expression said this all made sense to her.

"Comes with the territory," she muttered.

Then Lloyd's face fluttered into her mind.

"My dream's come true!"

I can never focus on any one thing, but he knows what he wants to be and worked toward that...and I went above and beyond to try and save him.

It felt like she'd only just come to terms with her own actions.

She looked back at the secretary, feeling the warmth of the evening wind brushing past her cheeks.

"Ever since I was a child, I wanted to be an actress."

"An actress?" The secretary looked momentarily surprised but quickly recovered. "I see. Very well, I'll arrange for some theater troupe to take you in. I have that power now..."

Kikyou shook her head. "But I can't do it. I'm not right for it. What I think always shows on my face."

And her face looked like she was staring at some foul thing. A moment later, she'd circled around behind him.

"What are you—?!"

"If you think my being an odd-jobs girl means I'll do *anything* for money, you're sorely mistaken! Hell, the whole reason I do this is because I don't want hardheaded, arrogant assholes like you telling me what to do!"

The secretary had not expected this invective from her at all. "I see," he said ruefully. "Let's find out if you still refuse once you see *this.*"

He began writhing as if ripples were running up his emaciated back—then something long and thin sprouted from its surface.

"Roots?" Kikyou yelped.

She didn't have time to dodge. They were already wrapped around her legs.

Kikyou could feel the strength leaving her body. Fatigue and weariness spread up her legs, and she couldn't fight the roots. They dragged her, lifted her up, and then slammed her to the ground.

Once that was done, the roots released her.

"Gah!" Kikyou gasped. All the air was knocked out of her lungs.

The secretary glared down at her. "With the amount of life energy I just absorbed from you, you won't be walking anywhere soon."

The roots wrapped around his body, making him look like a house abandoned for decades. Slowly, they took the form of a tree over six yards tall, with the man's tired face in the center of it.

The tree began moving, leaves rustling.

"Are you surprised? This is the treant power I've been harboring inside me, but not just any treant."

"So you're the one infected? No! I should have guessed whoever was responsible would do that to protect himself... Why didn't I think of that?"

"Now, back to our negotiations. My offer has changed. Obey me, or I'll turn you into fertilizer for my children! Once I've taken this form, there's no holding back."

"...Oh, geez."

Kikyou saw that boy's smile again.

He had such a gentle smile and such absurd physical strength...

He was immune to poison...and able to detect someone sneaking up behind him...

"What's the matter? Too frightened to speak? You hardly seem the type."

"......"

"Come, give me your answer! I'm not going to wait long."

"Shut up, I'm thinking."

"Oh, right, sorry."

Her voice had such steel behind it that the treant secretary reverted to old habits. He'd always been rather meek.

But Kikyou's mind was racing so fast she didn't even notice how pathetic he was.

Of course I never realized... I mean...I mean, that boy's obviously impossible!

She was going back over everything Lloyd had done. None of it was normal.

She'd assumed he was infected with a treant, but now that she knew it wasn't true, he was even more of a mystery.

"Is he even human?"

Based on the evidence she'd seen, she found herself deeply unsure.

"Heh-heh-heh, that's a difficult question," the secretary said. "In this form, I can hardly be called human anymore. Yet…I'm a new form of a life, a—"

"Quiet! I was talking to myself!"

"Oh, right, sorry."

The secretary's leaves rustled despondently.

As if she'd forgotten the urgency of her predicament, Kikyou turned to the half-tree secretary, speaking with the tone of a shopkeeper scolding a part-time worker.

"You only put that sapling in yourself?"

"Don't worry, this diabolical power is mine alone! But it is every bit as strong as—"

"Argh, then I'm back to square one! It would have been so simple if there had just been *two*! Go get a second one ready!"

"Oh, right, sorry?"

The secretary's roots rubbed together awkwardly. Even in this monstrous form, he couldn't keep his head up… She was starting to feel sorry for him.

Unsure why she was so mad at him, the secretary fell silent. These kinds of situations *were* hard to handle. He clearly had the advantage here, so why was she acting like this? His head tilted to one side inside the trunk.

Then there was a rustling noise… Someone was pushing through the brush.

Both turned to look.

"I could have sworn the chief landed this way…"

The boy with the gentle smile, Lloyd, stepped into the clearing, steam rising off of him, clearly tracing Alka's trajectory.

Still sweating from the bath, he looked like he was on a post-soak stroll…but Kikyou stared at him as if she were seeing a monster.

...Why is he...? No, he was just in the bath... How did he cover that much ground already?

It had only been a few minutes, and this was far enough away that she'd needed binoculars to see him. Since he wasn't infected by a treant, this was his natural ability...

A shiver ran down her spine.

Meanwhile, Lloyd was still toasty from the bath. He looked happy to see her.

"Oh, Kikyou! What's up? What brings you here? Did you see the chief come flying past? She's naked, so I'm worried she'll catch a cold."

If this "chief" had gone flying past naked, a cold seemed like the least of her problems...but that only fueled Kikyou's fear.

The secretary had been equally floored by this sudden arrival, but he recovered, showing his bizarre form and attempting to intimidate Lloyd.

"Hmm, and just who are—?"

"Who are you? Tell me the truth!"

Kikyou stole his line.

The secretary was getting rather upset. "I wanted to say that!" He rattled his leaves mournfully.

"Um...I'm Lloyd?" Lloyd was completely confused. Everyone here seemed to be on a different page entirely. "Did you forget me or something?"

"Oh, right!" the secretary said. "The bellboy who brought the meal alongside the hotel owner. But why are you—?"

"Why are you here?! Spit it out! How did you get here?! How did you cover that distance?!"

Once again, his line had been snatched away.

"Let me talk!" the secretary complained, another sad rustle running through his leaves. This whole treant parasite thing had been reduced to the goofiness of a kid forced to play a tree in the school play.

"Uh...I walked? But what's with this guy?"

Lloyd finally addressed the treant-infected secretary.

"Heh-heh-heh, curious, are you? Yes, as might well be expected! Behold my sinister form!"

"Oh, you're the secretary! How'd you end up like that? Wait..."

"Clever child—yes, I'm sure what you're thinking is correct. And you can imagine what's going to happen to you now."

"You're...preparing a party trick?"

"Yes! The illegal treant cultivation was all my— Huh?"

"It's a great concept! Dressing up as a cypress to impress Threonine—wow, it's really realistic!"

Lloyd's danger meter hovered at zero. He was stroking the secretary's bark as if petting a neighborhood cat or dog.

"To hell with him! What *are* you! Tell me the truth!"

"Uh? I'm just me? What's gotten into you, Kikyou? Did you follow up the magazine with a philosophy book?"

"That's... Ha-ha!"

First, Kikyou ignored him; then Lloyd dismissed him as a party trick—the secretary was at the end of his rope.

"I've given myself overwhelming power! I've become a new species! Getting treated like this...it's just not acceptable!"

His upper torso had remained largely intact, but the trunk was starting to swallow it up. Before he knew it, the secretary had grown much larger than the trees around him.

"You're— What the?! He's huge!" He heard a muffled voice through the trunk.

"Nobody ever notices me... They even forgot to bring me a moist towelette in the restaurant..."

Sounded like old traumas were digging into him, and he'd bottled all that up into pure hatred—a classic human failing! But this was hardly a laughing matter.

"Oh...*but that doesn't matter now. I am the Tree Demon Lord, the Erlking! I will cast off the shackles of the past, seek light and water, lay down roots, make myself a bed, and cover the world with my offspring!*"

"D-Demon Lord?" Kikyou squeaked.

"Too late to fear me now!"

True. Perhaps she should already have been afraid.

Following this muffled threat, the secretary-turned-Demon-Lord began extending his roots. They pulsed like pumps flushing something into the ground. A moment later, small treants hidden within the surrounding cypresses all began growing at once.

They tore their way out of their hiding spots, and in the blink of an eye, treants surrounded them.

The muted voice sounded pleased.

"I used all the nutrients I stored. The results are adequate...and where they aren't..."

"Oh, is this all part of the party trick? I know you want to make it real, but you can't go growing treants for *that*! It'll cause problems for the neighbors."

"Problems?! That's such an understatement!"

Lloyd looked like he was scolding someone for feeding stray cats. Kikyou's mind simply couldn't keep up with this, and her entire face was starting to twitch.

"Oh!" Lloyd said. "So that's why you're here, Kikyou! A guest was up to something, and you came to reprimand them!"

"Huh? What?"

Lloyd grinned, striking a pose—the one Kikyou had taught him.

"Don't worry! Cleaning up these weeds is my job!"

"Mwa-ha-ha! Weeds? Party tricks? I see, the fear has made you take leave of your—"

Lloyd punched through a nearby treant.

"—senses...but...but this makes no sense... Oh, crap!"

As Lloyd dispatched treant after treant, it became clear that the Demon Lord was the one who should be afraid.

In very little time, Lloyd had cleaned up all the treants in the area.

Fear had Kikyou paralyzed—she simply couldn't process the situation. She just watched Lloyd go at it, her jaw hanging open.

"If we don't need to harvest the wood, even I can handle this!"

Treants were a common source of firewood in Kunlun, but the only way to ensure treants left lumber behind was to defeat them before they noticed you. In other words, in Kunlun, "gathering firewood" was a stealth mission. If you defeated the creatures *after* they noticed you...

Pshhht.

"The treants... They're turning into smoke..."

...they would vanish, leaving behind only a pile of ash that twinkled in the moonlight, turning over earth where the roots had been yanked out.

"Definitely no firewood left... The villagers would all laugh at me."

"...Lloyd...just who are you?"

"I'm Lloyd Belladonna! A military cadet of Azami— Wait, where'd the secretary go?"

"......He's gone! No...!"

Kikyou quickly scanned the area, looking for any sign of the Demon Lord. In the distance, she could hear trees falling over—in the direction of the hotel.

"He said something about being low on nutrients... That's really bad!"

Kikyou tried to pursue, but with her life energy drained, she couldn't move.

Lloyd saw her struggling and gently put his arms around her.

"Don't force yourself. I'll take care of it."

"But everyone in the hotel will—"

"Yes...if he starts running around the hotel at night dressed like that, we'll be flooded with complaints! That wouldn't be good at all."

Kikyou gaped at him, flashing him a look that said he was way off base.

"I'm only here for the weekend, but I'm also a cadet. I've always dreamed about being useful to people—so leave this to me. I know I don't seem all that reliable, but..."

Kikyou listened to him quietly.

"...if I do my best when people need me, then I think someday people will come to appreciate it. I've always been a wimp, never confident in anything but housework, but I did my best to cook, clean, or do anything else I thought I was capable of, and I'm starting to find my way forward. I may still be just an inexperienced cadet, but one day... I'll be a proper soldier, and—"

There was a loud crash from the hotel. They could see the Treant Demon Lord, even bigger than before. Nearly a dozen yards tall, it was growing uglier and uglier.

Lloyd's eyes widened at the sheer size of it.

"Wow, at a time like this? A monster?! Is this because I was fighting?"

No, Lloyd, it was the secretary. And he wasn't just a monster.

He was a Demon Lord.

"About the rumors of illegal treant cultivation… You're not about to tell me the treant lumber I'm purchasing from the Lidocaine family was cultivated illegally, are you?"

"What?" Threonine squawked. "You're buying that from us?"

"Yes—there was a chance my daughter might become part of your family, so I was hoping to alleviate that concern here."

"So you and Threonine *are* responsible for the illegal cultivation that's led to these comas?" Coba bristled, ready to go after Threonine again.

But Selen's father restrained him. "Now, now, let's not jump to conclusions. This has been bothering me for some time."

Coba couldn't conceal his surprise—Selen's father had stopped him quite easily.

"A-are you…a martial artist of some kind?" he asked.

"I'm embarrassed to admit it," Selen's father replied, turning his eyes to the floor. "But this is for my daughter."

"Your daughter?"

"The Cursed Belt Princess…you've heard of her? That was my Selen. We were told it would take considerable power to remove the belt, so…I spent some time training."

He rolled up his sleeve, revealing wiry muscles underneath.

"Bulking up too much would intimidate people, interfering with business, so…anyway, Selen's belt was removed in Azami, so all this muscle is going to waste now."

Sheepishly, he rolled his sleeve back down.

"S-so," Threonine said. "The marriage arrangement wasn't a trick?"

"A trick? No, nothing like that. Now that her curse is lifted, there's no reason to have her in the army. It would never do for her to get injured in service…and I've heard rumors of a dangerous stalker in the country. I decided it was best to arrange a marriage at once."

Those rumors were probably about his daughter.

"...Thanks to that cursed belt, the other local lords look down on us. Only the Lidocaine family agreed to consider the arrangement."

Selen's father bowed his head low.

"O-oh...that explains it..."

Threonine had only taken him up on the offer to obtain info on the illegal cultivation, so this left him feeling rather guilty.

"And as we've conducted business here repeatedly, it seemed like the best choice for the prospective couple to meet. I was hoping to verify the cultivation was legitimate while I was at it."

"No, wait, wait. This is all news to me! You're sure you're buying the lumber from us?"

"Yes, from a young man who identified himself as an agent of the Lidocaine family...although this does explain some inconsistencies, Threonine. It was odd that the representative kept insisting I know who I was dealing with. I wondered if you were drunk."

"I know nothing of this. I'm telling the truth!"

The conversation was going nowhere fast, but just then, the restaurant doors slammed open, and a large man appeared carrying a pot.

"Who made this soup?!" he roared.

It was Allan. He'd recovered from the numbing effect of the treant balm in the soup and now was here to complain.

Coba and Threonine. The two burly men took one glance at each other and then glared at Allan.

Allan saw his father with a large crowd, clearly in the middle of something.

"...Sorry to interrupt!" he said, trying to quietly back away.

But Threonine stopped him.

"Are you responsible?"

"Responsible for what, Dad?"

Allan was lost enough already without having baseless accusations leveled at him. There were tears in his eyes.

"I knew it made no sense! My fool of a son, the toast of the Azami army? You bought your way up with the money you raised selling treant wood!"

"What the hell are you talking about, Dad? I'm doing my best!"

Marie, confused to see someone she knew clutching a soup pot in a bathrobe, called out, "Allan! What are you wearing?!"

"Er...Marie! Why are you here?"

"I could ask the same! And...why the pot?"

Allan glared down at the pot balefully.

"Listen to this! I drank some of this soup, and my entire body went numb! I thought I was gonna die! I'm gonna give the chef a piece of my mind if it's the last thing—"

"...Sorry."

"It's not your fault, Marie!"

It totally was, but while she hung her head, Selen's father decided he should calm Threonine down.

"No, Threonine, not that boy. The one I met had a dark tan..."

"What? Then...who...?"

A scream arose from the crowd. Someone was pointing out the window. Coba turned to look and saw...

"What the hell is that? A tree monster?! A treant!"

The giant secretary was rushing toward them.

Coba grabbed a phone, calling the front desk. "Hey, it's me! Sound the alarm! There's a giant tree monster headed this way!"

"Dammit! The sapling matured! Kikyou failed?!" Threonine wailed.

"...Selen!" her father shouted, looking anxious. But his voice was drowned out in screams.

"Argh," Marie wailed. "Get the hell out of the bath and come back here, you tiny hag!"

"Calm down!" Allan cried. "Don't push! Keep it orderly!"

Swearing under her breath, Marie began helping Allan guide the crowd out of the restaurant.

"Dammit! We need to evacuate the place," Coba swore. "First these comas, now they're after my hotel... I *will* have you arrested for this!"

But Coba's voice was lost in the high-pitched shriek of the hotel alarms.

* * *

While alarms echoed through the halls, Selen, Riho, Phyllo, and Mena were standing on the roof of a souvenir shop near the lake. They'd been staring in the direction Alka had been thrown and saw the treant rise up out of the woods and go on the attack. They'd hastily dressed and rushed to intercept.

"Up close, it's even bigger." Riho gulped. "Damn, where'd this thing come from? There'd better be a reward…"

The sight of the creature silhouetted against the moon was enough to frighten even her.

"Calm down. Stick to the plan, and we'll be fine," Mena said, her voice much lower than usual. The other three listened intently. "First, the bait—someone needs to lure it away from the hotel toward the lake."

Mena pointed toward the dock where boat rentals were moored. It was a decently open space that offered a few buildings to stand on and appeared tailor-made for flinging big spells around.

"Then, I'll bind it with water magic—but I dunno how long I can hold down a Treant Demon Lord. Before I try, Riho, charge your mithril arm with a fire spell and hit it hard."

"Roger that. What happens after you bind it?"

"The weak point is the core—the living thing it absorbed. We'll have to attack that. But there's a strong chance the core will be immune to magic, so that's where Phyllo comes in."

"……Mm." Phyllo nodded.

"Of course, it may not be so easily bound and might not die just because we hit the core once, but we just have to hold on long enough for Lloyd or the chief to get back."

"Yeah, if either of them comes back, we'll be fine," Riho said, doing warm-up stretches. "Right. I'll be on top of that tree there. Good luck!"

"……Mm."

Riho and Phyllo turned to go.

"Wait!" Selen yelped. "I heard her say 'bait,' but she wasn't specific!"

"Well, Selen, no time to waste!"

"No, no, no, no! Why am *I* bait?! That's perfect for someone as durable as Phyllo!"

"You've got the cursed belt auto-guard! And you can use that to yank yourself onto roofs or into trees if need be," Mena explained.

"I heard you hooked it onto a chandelier to throw yourself into Lloyd's arms earlier today! You're turning into a monster!" Riho called out to her.

Selen groaned, but Phyllo patted her gently on the back.

"...Don't worry."

"Phyllo! Will you take over for me?"

"...I'll gather your bones."

"That's worse than what I'd feared! You want me dying?!"

"...You threw yourself into my master's arms? ...How indecent."

"You got drunk and did way worse! You're far more indecent than I am!"

The ground shook. The Treant Demon Lord's roots were writhing, and it was picking up speed.

"We're outta time! Positions, everyone!"

"Mm."

"Good luck, m'lady!"

"And the day started off so lovely! Argh, fine! I'll show you all what I can do!"

Grumbling, Selen dashed off after them, headed toward the shore.

There was a lot of gravel around the lake that crunched under Selen's feet as she ran. She reached the spot Mena had indicated and stopped.

"Yoo-hoo! Massive tree! Come this way!" she yelled at the top of her lungs.

"You tell him, Selen! You gotta be even meaner if you want him to take the bait!" Riho called from a tree nearby.

"Hngg... Y-you're an idiot! I think!"

"Is that your best smack talk? Only the brokenhearted would call someone an idiot on a lakeshore! You gotta really twist that knife!"

Riho seemed much better at insults.

"What does 'smack talk' even mean?! I wish it was you doing this..."

Selen rummaged through her vocabulary, doing her best to taunt the giant tree.

"Um...you're ginormous! Really slow! And dumb! A big dummy!"

"They're starting to overlap a bit! Point deduction!"

"Big talk for someone in a tree! You half-wit! You human failure! You're um...um...bald!"

The treant had been ignoring her, relentlessly moving toward the hotel, but at this last comment, it swung sharply in her direction.

"I just have a big forehead!"

That sharply receding hairline had definitely been bothering him. The Treant Demon Lord charged at Selen.

"Aughhhh! It's after me! Riho! Mena! Heeeeelp! Please!"

Selen broke into a headlong run, not a glance in either direction.

"Heh-heh-heh! Payback for all the good times you helped yourself to earlier!" Riho said. Then her smile faded. "Right...my part's up next."

She turned to the approaching tree, deploying a spell. Her mithril arm began gleaming.

"An inferno in my hand..."

That was when the unexpected happened.

"*Fl*— Yikes!"

Before she could yell *"Flame"* and complete the incantation, something stabbed through the air where she'd been. She barely managed to scramble aside in time.

"That's was close... Were those...leaves?"

Watching from a distance, Mena swore. "*Tch*... An auto-guard that reacts to magic power?"

As a test, Mena tried using a small fire spell, and the creature didn't miss a beat—a giant branch swung and sent leaves flying her way.

"Yikes! Crap! It even reacts to short chants!"

As Mena was starting to realize magic wasn't an option, Phyllo ran past Selen and kicked the giant tree.

"————Hah!"

Thud... It made a loud noise, but the treant didn't slow at all.

"……Then a combo."

Phyllo rained blows on it, which might have slowed it slightly, but they definitely didn't stop its advance.

Grimacing, Riho ransacked her pockets, looking for options.

"Crap…we're gonna take too much damage before Lloyd gets here… There's gotta be something…"

But the only thing in her pockets was the free book of matches she'd found in her room.

"Damn, that won't be enough… It's fire, sure, but…"

A match wasn't exactly going to do any real damage. And while Riho weighed her options, the treant's roots crept toward her.

"Riho! At your feet!"

"Crap!"

Roots were sprouting up beneath her. She quickly dodged, grabbing the tree's trunk.

Her vision was immediately filled with treant roots, whooshing through the space she'd been and chasing her up the trunk.

"Damn… It's gonna take out one foothold after another… Go away!"

She was dodging the onslaught for now, but the tendrils showed no signs of tiring.

"How can I get out of this? I can't use magi— Augh!"

Riho had jumped to avoid the roots, and they'd swept sideways, sending her flying through the air. She'd been nearly at the top of the tree, so this was going to be a long fall—one that could easily prove fatal. Even as she fell, though, Riho's mind was in overdrive.

Something was running toward them from the hotel at tremendous speed. It was…

"Neigh!"

A horse? The horse Riho had groomed so carefully was dragging a wagon after it, right under her falling body.

Poof! The soft canopy of the high-end wagon caught Riho safely.

"A canopy? I'm saved…and you're…!"

"Neigh!" (Translation: "Sorry I'm late!")

It was a beautiful black horse with intense eyes.

"Weren't you in a pen…? Augh!"

Riho looked toward the stables, spying a broken fence and the horses she'd looked after…all looking rather red-faced.

They'd worked together to break out and help her.

"…Okay, I love horses again!"

Riho hopped off the canopy and gave the horse's mane a good rub.

"Mm? What's that smell?"

It was a distinctive, oily odor.

She followed the scent and checked inside the canopy…and gaped.

"Bottle bombs?!"

Three whole cases of them. The horse's charge had knocked a few over, and the inside of the carriage was soaked in volatile oil.

"M'lady… You bought waaaay too much. Heh."

But just this once, she'd done a good job. Just this once. Riho picked up a case and started running toward the treant.

"…Mm!"

Meanwhile, Phyllo was fending off a vicious root attack somehow, clearly about to reach her limit.

"…Each strike is weak, but…there are…so many…"

If she splintered one, another would hit from the side, and if she deflected that, from above, below, in front of her—roots flew toward her from every direction.

"…If it would just flinch…"

…then she could put her back into a big hit and knock it down, but the onslaught didn't give her time.

"Phyllo! You okay?" Selen called out.

"…Not really… I need an opening…"

Then something exploded at the center of the treant.

"Magic? I thought you couldn't chant!"

Both turned to see raging flames…and hear glass shattering, followed by another explosion.

"…Bottle bombs… Very powerful ones…"

Phyllo sounded almost shocked. Normal bottle bombs didn't explode like this. Even someone as stoic as Phyllo was surprised. These used a combination of special oils and magic stones, proving to be far more powerful than those known to mortals. Behold the terrifying power of Kunlun…well, of Shouma, anyway.

"Who the…?"

Both turned to see where the bottle bombs were coming from.

"Serves you right, rotten treant! Time for some slash and burn!"

Riho was gleefully applying matches to the bottles and flinging them at the creature. If you tried slash-and-burn agriculture with these napalm-esque bombs, you'd transform the land so badly, no one would ever want to farm it.

"…"

The sight of Riho in full-on terrorist mode left Phyllo and Selen momentarily stunned.

"…We can win this," Phyllo said, seeing the onslaught dying down. She dashed between some roots, approaching the trunk. "…Hmph. Hah!"

Putting her back into it, she hit the treant with her strongest kick, knocking it off balance.

Thud. Thud. Thud…

The treant staggered, flailing its roots frantically to keep from falling over.

"*Tch*, it still isn't going down. Aah!"

The enemy had suddenly jumped, like an old drunk avoiding a fall by abruptly transitioning into a backflip. The comparison isn't far off, given the age of the secretary inside the thing…

But the landing didn't go so well. Off balance, the treant was forced to grab the hotel for support.

"…That's…the restaurant," Phyllo warned.

"Father!" Selen yelled.

Before she could think twice, she was racing toward the building.

Inside the restaurant, Marie's murder mystery dinner party had ended—rather forcibly—in a shower of rubble and dust. The guests looked up to find the wall caved in and a giant, dubiously colored tree leaning against the hotel.

"A-augh! M-my hotel! We only just renovated!" Coba wailed.

"Damn… How dare you… My family is heavily decorated! On the honor of Threonine Toin Lidocaine, this shall not stand!"

Threonine picked up a nearby chair, ready to charge the treant.

"No, don't! That's just a chair! This thing is dangerous! Keep your distance!" Marie called, but her warning fell on deaf ears.

She tried to grab Threonine, but he brushed her off.

"Unhand me! That thing besmirched the Lidocaine name, and I'm gonna make it pay!"

"Dad! It's not safe! Stay back!" yelled Allan.

Threonine threw the chair, but the treant's bark was like iron. The chair bounced off harmlessly.

"Lord Threonine! We'd better retreat and let the police handle this!"

"Dammit! Where'd my secretary go?" Threonine roared. "He's supposed to be fetching the police! How long is that damn fool going to keep us waiting?"

At this, the side of the treant's trunk opened up, and the secretary's face loomed over them.

"You called?"

"""""............"""""

A deathly silence settled over the scene, like when the best man's speech turns out to be about the groom's philandering.

"Y-you?!" Threonine croaked at last. "What does this mean? Did the treant take control of you?!"

"No," the secretary said.

"Th-then why are you inside it?!"

"Because I'm the one who was illegally cultivating the treants!"

This silenced Threonine completely.

"You had no idea, did you? You never do! You pay no attention to your subordinates, always trying to do everything yourself. That's why I concocted this plan! As long as I didn't get caught, I'd get rich—and if I did get caught, I could pin it all on you!"

"That's no reason to do something this stupid!"

"Stupid? I agree! But how could you understand how it feels to have no future? Threonine—I'm going to consume you now."

A treant root shot toward Threonine, trying to run him through.

"Look out!" Allan shoved his father out of the way, then wrapped his arms around the root, holding it still. "Run, Dad! Hraghh!"

"Fool! I'll just drain your life away!"

A faint light wreathed around the root Allan was clutching, siphoning his strength. He staggered but managed to remain on his feet, throwing off the root and recovering.

"Allan! Are you okay?" Marie asked.

"A little dizzy," Allan said, grimacing. "But I'm tough enough to handle it! And they don't teach cadets in Azami to abandon unarmed civilians in a time of need."

"A-Allan..."

"Yeah, I'm a screwup, and I ain't too bright—but I'm not scared of monsters anymore."

Allan had once been great at fighting people but too afraid to go up against monsters. He'd entered Azami's military with the goal of getting promoted before anyone made him fight monsters.

Threonine had been well aware of this, and it was a big part of his contempt for his son. "I see," he whispered, clearly regretting his harshness. "You've grown."

"And I know my master won't abandon us at a time like this!" Allan grinned.

The secretary at the treant's core scowled.

"Out of the way! Let me kill that man!"

"Hell no! I've been trained to do the opposite! I'm Allan the Axman, and I'm gonna chop your ass down!"

Allan reached for his back, trying to grab his favorite ax...and... came up with empty air.

"Ah! I'm unarmed!"

Allan had been wearing nothing but a bathrobe ever since he collapsed in the sauna, but only now did he realize it.

"..."

There was an awkward silence.

"Die!"

"Hang on! They didn't teach us how to fight monsters bare-handed! Dammit!"

"I knew my son was an idiot!" Threonine roared.

Allan desperately dodged the treant's attacks and started throwing anything he could get his hands on. Chairs. Tables. Paintings from the walls. And...

"Take that! And that! And that!"

"Ha-ha-ha! What a clown!"

Allen threw the soup pot he'd brought with him. Balm-infused soup splattered the creature.

"Ha-ha-ha...ha?" The secretary's muffled laugh faded. He felt a wave of heat spreading through him. Steam began gushing out of his body.

"Ha? Ha? Ha?"

He lost his balance, staggering against the hotel, then toppling over backward.

Whumm...

The Treant Demon Lord withered away, as if its core had been removed. Its branches and leaves drooped toward the ground.

"...Seriously, who made that soup? That's *definitely* not fit for human consumption!"

"Ah-ha-ha, seriously... What was in that herbal paste?" Marie asked, standing right next to him. Her laugh sounded very hollow.

But the giant root receding from the projectile soup seemed to have actually calmed everyone down.

"The leaves are withering! Riho! Now's our chance! Hit it with ice after my water spell!" Mena yelled.

"Ice?" Riho confirmed. "Oh, I get it!"

She stopped throwing bottle bombs and jumped on the horse.

"Unhitch the wagon, and...you ready to go?"

"Whinny." (Translation: "You betcha.")

The horse shook its mane for emphasis, and Riho gave it a rub in return.

"Your real talent has been wasted pulling wagons around, huh? Right, on my signal, do a quick lap of the treant."

"Whinny." (Translation: "No problem.")

As Riho and the horse conferred, all the water in the lake began to spray, gathering together.

"Time to take out my frustrations!" Mena said. With the situation in their favor, her tone had regained its usual impishness. *"Water Snake!"*

As Mena finished her spell, the mass of lake water took the shape of a cobra, which slithered across the lake's surface, headed for the treant.

When it reached is target, it wrapped around the withering plant.

"Right, let's go!" Riho snapped the reins, and the horse whinnied in reply. It galloped swiftly around the treant while Riho held her mithril arm aloft.

"Diamond Dust!"

Ice shards chilled the air around her, then began rocketing toward the treant. They shattered against it as the horse ran a second lap. In no time, the area was filled with soft rime.

"Got it!" Riho cheered.

"Don't jinx it!" Mena yelled. "It's still alive! The core ain't exposed! We gotta do something about that, or...!"

Roots were crawling out from beneath the immobilized treant.

"Damn, this thing don't give up!"

"It can't move, but it'll start draining life from everything around it! Find that core and destroy it!"

"The final stretch! Let's do this!" Riho roared.

The horse let out its loudest whinny so far.

Selen reached the area around the restaurant at top speed.

The collapsed treant had limply backed away, drained of color, like a flower someone had forgotten to water.

While Selen had been running, Mena's and Riho's spells had gone off, immobilizing the monster. Selen was relieved, but the restaurant was in such bad condition, she couldn't entirely relax.

"Did everyone get away safe?"

She used her belt to nimbly hoist herself to the restaurant level. There was a terraced area, a sort of outdoor café. The night wind blew past deserted tables and chairs, knocking them together.

"This area seems fine...but where's my father?"

Selen's eyes locked on what looked like an exposed wine cellar. The wall had collapsed, and blood-colored spirits were staining the floor.

She found her father lying there, buried beneath barrels and rubble. The floor had opened up, swallowing him.

"Father!"

Hearing his daughter's voice, he answered, his voice barely a whisper. "That you, Selen...?"

"Father! I'll get you out of there!"

Selen began frantically moving furniture out of the way, but the wine casks and rubble were too heavy for her to budge.

"...You can't. Just...get to safety."

His breathing was ragged, which only made her more desperate.

"What are you talking about? If we don't get out, you—"

"Divine retribution... I should never have tried to force this marriage on you..."

"Don't try to talk!"

"...I'm really glad the belt's curse was lifted. It had been so long since I'd seen you...I didn't know what to say."

"..." Selen said nothing, desperately trying to move the debris.

"What are those...roots?!"

Flailing against its bondage, the treant's roots had spread out, searching for life energy. Seeking the power it needed to free itself, it was after anything and everything.

One root noticed them and came writhing in their direction.

"Tch!" Selen fought it off with rapier and belt, but when she deflected it, it just tried to go around her to grab her father.

Again, her belt went wild, stopping it, but more roots came, surrounding the collapsed wine cellar.

"Go! Forget about me...," her father rasped.

Selen spoke quietly but firmly.

"There's a boy I'm in love with. He always insists that he's weak, but helps people with a smile."

She spoke of the boy who'd released her from the curse that had left her face wrapped in a hideous belt, who'd saved not just her, but Marie and Riho as well.

"I want to be a soldier to help people, like in my favorite novel."

Slashing at the advancing roots with her belt, Selen narrowed her eyes.

"I want to see the world as he does!" she yelled. "If he says he wants to save everyone, then I want to, too! That's why I'm a cadet in Azami! And Selen Hemein will *not* give up!"

"Selen..."

Between her rapier and the belt, Selen was doing everything in her power, but there was only so much she could do to protect someone who couldn't move.

"...!"

Her knees buckled, and she staggered.

"Not yet... Not yet!"

Just as all seemed lost...

"Sorry I'm late!"

Like a gust of wind slicing through the night air, a boy appeared...in a simple linen shirt and canvas pants, with russet hair and gentle eyes.

"...Oh!"

He looked just as he had when she'd first reached Azami, the day he'd saved her.

"Are you okay?" he asked, smiling. "You're not hurt, are you?"

"...No! I'm just like you, Lloyd! I'm a military cadet! I can handle a little punishment!"

Lloyd grinned wider, then kicked aside the roots nearby—literally sent them all flying with a single kick.

The roots crumbled, filling the air with an earthen smell. Selen was used to Lloyd's prowess, but her father was gaping. As most people would.

Seeing Selen's father trapped, Lloyd lifted the barrels off of him like they were made of paper.

"You're…the boy from the marriage arrangement? Lloyd, was it?"

"I owe you an explanation on that one. Later, though! Selen, get your father to safety! I'll…"

His eyes glinted, focusing on the bound treant.

"I'll go defeat that monster!"

Actually, it was a Demon Lord.

"Lloyd!"

A familiar voice came from the crack in the floor. Lloyd looked up.

"Marie?"

He took a quick hop, landing one floor up…and found more familiar faces.

"Oh! Lloyd!"

"Owner! You're okay? And, Allan! You're feeling better?"

"Lloyd?! What are *you* doing here?"

Threonine, meanwhile, couldn't believe someone had just jumped between floors.

"L-Lloyd? Who *are* you?"

"Don't worry! I'm just a part-time bellboy, but I'm *also* a military cadet from Azami!"

"You're…with Azami?"

"I'm just getting started, but we've been trained not to abandon anyone in a time of need!"

"Lloyd, listen, we've weakened the treant. Now we just need to hit the core…"

Threonine reacted with horror. "What? He may be good at jumping, but you can't ask a child… Right, Lloyd?"

"Huh? I can do it."

"Lloyd!" Threonine grabbed his shoulders. "Don't be ridiculous! Look how far it is!"

The creature was roughly a hundred yards from the restaurant. No normal jump could carry him that distance.

"Anyone can leap that far," Lloyd stated, as if it was obvious.

"Lloyd," Marie said. "It's almost down. Everyone weakened it for you, so..."

"Got it! I'll do my best! I think I can beat a treant-like monster."

"No, no, wait...er, what?"

Without even a running start, Lloyd leaped.

He rocketed through the air like he had wings, directly toward the fallen treant.

"What? Magic? Is that magic? Is he a mage?!"

"Afraid not, Threonine. That kid's no mage. That's pure physical strength," Coba said calmly.

"Dad! That's my master! The one who helped me get past my fear of monsters!"

"Your master... Him?!"

Before Threonine could recover, Lloyd landed on the treant trunk. He scrambled up and placed his ear against the bark.

"Hmm...in here?"

He began easily peeling the bark away. Everyone watching looked relieved.

"Lloyd's here! We've won against this thing now," Riho said, petting her horse.

"Been a while since I went on a ride that exhilarating," Mena joked, her old self again.

"...Mm," Phyllo said, extending a thumbs-up.

"..." Selen just gazed in wordless rapture.

As his friends watched, Lloyd finished peeling back the steel-like bark and began tunneling into the trunk like it was made of tofu.

Finally, he dragged out the gray core—the petrified secretary.

"Is this it? Okay! Let's do this! Hah!"

One mighty swing, and a crack ran up the Demon Lord's torso.

As it did, the treant's trunk turned to dust, swirling through the night sky.

Like stardust returning home, the dust drifted upward. It was a beautiful sight.

And where the treant had been…remained the secretary, covered in sap. Like a middle-aged man freshly hatched from an egg, he was dripping with goo—a rather hideous display.

Lloyd looked puzzled to find the secretary here, but then he looked down at the sap on his own fist.

"It really only took a single punch! I guess I really hogged all the glory, huh…"

He clenched his fist again, clearly pleased with himself.

"But I beat my first monster! With *my* friends, even I can do it!"

It wasn't a monster! It was a Demon Lord! Well, this wasn't the time or the place to point that out.

"With friends, nothing is too difficult!"

This experience was a valuable one for Lloyd.

A scene away from those friends for now… Back to the lakeside.

Alka awoke to the sensation of cold ground.

"Hmm?"

She appeared to be buried. The cold was all around her. And she was naked. Alka tried to figure out how she'd ended up like this.

"Did Marie bury me as payback for her daily struggles?"

She then heard a cheery voice from above.

"'Sup, Chief," he said. He was a tan young man, dressed like a delivery boy, looking down at her from a treetop.

Alka frowned up at him. "Shouma… Where have you been?"

"Mm? All over." He brushed off with a shrug. Then he laughed. "Ah-ha-ha. I've been all over the world, but you're the only person I've ever seen lying on the ground naked, sound asleep! Didn't want you catching cold, so I buried you there."

"*You* did this? You never did treat me with any respect!"

"Yeah, sorry! You're too dumb to catch a cold. Also…" His pleasant

©Nao Watanuki

smile never wavered, but his tone got real low, with genuine anger behind it. "You can't die, 'cause you're immortal."

"Where'd you hear *that*? Not…!"

Shouma peered at her surprised expression through some sort of tube. "Mm, lovely! How passionate!"

"You've teamed up with that man? You know working with him could spell the end of the human race!"

"What's wrong with that?! The destruction of mankind! What an exciting twist!"

The gentle smile only made Shouma seem all the more frightening. Alka let out a long sigh and flexed.

The ground shook, cracking open. Nearby animals fled as if from an earthquake.

"Whoops, if I let you catch me here, my plans will be ruined!" Shouma turned to leave. "The treants worked out well enough, but that Demon Lord attracted way too much attention! Wish these extras would stop showing off, seriously! Well, now that the Holy Sword's been pulled, there's plenty of other ways."

"What are you planning on using that sword for?! You fool!"

Alka scrambled out of the ground, but Shouma was already gone.

"You'll find out, Chief! It'll be real passionate! Say hi to Lloyd for me!"

Only his voice drifted from the forest depths.

Brushing mud off her bare form, Alka glared grimly after him.

"Shouma… Why would you work with *him*? *Achoo!*"

The serious vibe was totally ruined.

An Unnatural Explanation: Suppose You Blamed Everything on the Supernatural, Like in Edo-Period Japan

Warm sunlight was streaming through the windows of the hotel's unadorned offices.

Coba had been sleeping on his desk, but the light and the sounds of birds singing roused him.

"…Mm? Damn, I fell asleep here?"

The events of the night before had found Coba checking the safety of his guests and personally apologizing to each of them. He'd left the rest of the cleanup to Lloyd and his regular staff and thrown himself into incident reports and detailed damage claims for the police. At some point along the way, sleep had gotten the better of him.

His drool had smeared the letters on the document he'd been in the middle of. "I'll have to rewrite this one," he muttered, balling it up and hurling it at a nearby trash can.

He glanced at the clock and saw he still had time before breakfast. Relieved, he forced himself to his feet, headed for the lounge. In his head, he was still trying to figure out where they could serve breakfast with the restaurant in ruins, how to handle the fallout, where to take things next, etc.

"Not the way I'd hoped the holiday weekend would go… Hmm?"

Coba's bleary eyes had found Threonine, Kikyou, and the hotel staff all facing the same direction, mouths open, as if they couldn't believe their eyes.

More trouble? More treants? Coba raced over, and what he saw made his jaw drop, too.

"...Owner."

"...Lord Threonine. What on earth is going on?"

As if the conflict between them had never existed, they glanced at each other once, then back at the sight before them.

Their eyes were fixed on the restaurant the treant had demolished.

But somehow—it wasn't. Everything was exactly as it had been, as if nothing had ever happened to it. No—it was actually improved, as if it had opened right after remodeling.

Even more astonishing were the guests. Visitors whose anger had forced Coba into a never-ending stream of apologies the night before, guests who'd been left quivering with fear—were streaming into the restaurant as if nothing had happened.

"No clue. I'm as surprised as your staff."

Then, a boy with a gentle smile poked his head out of the kitchen. It was Lloyd. He saw the other staff all lined up, even though they hadn't been ordered to.

"Morning, everyone!" he greeted them.

An array of distinct faces appeared behind him.

"Man, I'm bushed!" said a little girl in a white robe—Alka. She yawned and stretched, grumbling to herself. "Spent all night erasing guests' memories one at a time *and* casting repair spells on the broken building!"

"Shh...don't tell them that! What if they demand a detailed explanation?" Marie asked, putting her pointy hat back on. "Plus, this is all your fault for vanishing while the Demon Lord was rampaging. It was a real nightmare!"

"Haven't done much cooking in a while, but at least we got breakfast ready on time!"

"...Mm."

The Quinone sisters, Mena and Phyllo, both had suspicious traces of sauce around their lips. Clearly, they'd been snacking.

"You both just stood there eating!" Riho snapped. "I mean...Lloyd basically did everything, so not like I was much better, but at least I set some tables!"

"Heh-heh-heh. *I* help Lloyd in the meal hall all the time, so I did the most here!" Allan boasted, drying his hands on his apron. It looked rather good on him, really.

"Cooking with Sir Lloyd… Basically, proof of marriage!" Selen moaned blissfully.

Everyone else present just gaped at them.

"Owner, we got the restaurant fixed up early, so we threw ourselves into making breakfast and managed it all in time somehow!" Lloyd explained.

"But…," Coba said, frowning. "The place was totally demolished… You repaired it overnight? And the customers don't remember anything that happened… How?"

Marie and Alka looked at each other, whispering.

"See? I told you! Using spells that ridiculous will just arouse suspicion!"

"But I had to! Here I am in a lovely hotel! I don't want to eat on some trashed terrace surrounded by gloomy folk!"

"Then don't be so lazy and erase memories of the staff, too!"

"When did you get so drastic, Marie? I don't know who you get that from."

It was almost certainly from Alka.

What conclusion did Coba and his staff reach after observing this?

"Well, this is Lloyd we're talking about! Of course he got it done!"

Their faith in Lloyd was tantamount to abandonment of all thought. Once Coba broke the silence, the rest of the crew chimed in, filling the air with praise for Lloyd.

"Yeah, of course Lloyd handled it!"

"I'm sure he did such a good job apologizing to the guests that they all forgave everything! I certainly would!"

"Lloyd could do a fist pump, and everything would go back to normal!"

Riho shook her head. "This is beyond trust. They're starting a new religion around him…"

These people were ready to pay a premium for water hand-pumped by Lloyd.

While Threonine was still recovering, the border police approached.

"Lord Threonine, we heard there was a treant rampage...but the building seems intact."

"Hmm, the whole area was reduced to rubble, but this magnificent boy repaired it overnight."

"...You seem tired," one police officer said, clearly concluding that Threonine wasn't thinking straight.

"And the culprit...?"

"He's locked up in the wine cellar. I'm afraid my secretary was responsible," Threonine revealed, with great regret.

"R-really? I thought you suspected the owner?"

"It's true, I'm afraid. I jumped to conclusions and failed to keep proper tabs on my own affairs. I will accept responsibility for these failings upon my return. This way."

He led the police toward the wine cellar.

Coba watched them go. Threonine paused to bow one last time.

"Owner...Coba Lamin. I apologize for casting unwarranted suspicion on you."

"Raise your head, sir. I suspected you, as well...so we're even."

But Threonine kept his head down.

"No, my failure to control my subordinates and my bias against Azami are directly responsible for this disaster."

"That's enough of that. All our hotel asks is that you continue to grace us with your company."

Faced with this display of humility, Threonine raised his head and clasped hands with Coba.

"After everything I said, you still forgive me. Thank you, sir. It seems I had the wrong idea about the army of Azami! I promise I'll stay here again—and this time for pleasure, not business."

"We look forward to it."

As the two exchanged a firm handshake, Kikyou nodded to herself nearby.

"Good, good! All's well that ends well. Make sure you pay me well, Threonine!"

Threonine gave her a suspicious look.

"Kikyou… What did you actually *do*?"

"Huh?"

"Turns out my secretary was the one the treant infected, so you were not only wrong about that, you let him go berserk. And it was your reports that made me suspect Coba in the first place."

"Wha— Uh…I didn't report… W-well, I did suspect the wrong person of being infected, but…"

As Kikyou stammered, Coba took a firm grip on her shoulders.

"I hear you're actually a spy Threonine hired, Kikyou."

"I—I was… Uh, sorry for all the deception, but… That hurts?"

"I don't mind forgiving all that—but you skipped out on *far* too much work! And half of that had nothing to do with spying."

"I—I was laying the groundwork to avoid suspicion!"

"Owner," Threonine said, turning to Coba. "As her employer, I give you permission to work her as long as you please. Consider it my way of repaying you."

"Accepted!"

"What?!" Kikyou yelped. "I've got nothing to repay!"

"And you'll get no pay from me until Coba's satisfied! Time to stop being useless!"

"You'll work off every minute you slacked…and with no spying to do, there'll be *no* more slacking!"

"You're delaying payment?! That makes this just a part-time job! That blows!"

Coba dragged her away.

"So Kikyou's back to work," Lloyd said. "I knew she was a hard worker—we can all learn from her!"

His perception of her as a serious veteran coworker had never once wavered.

Once Kikyou was out of sight, Threonine turned to his son.

"Allan, you've really grown. You used to be so scared of monsters. I never thought I'd see the day you could manage all that unarmed."

"D-Dad!"

"When you enlisted in the military, I was concerned for the Lidocaine name and reputation…but it seems you've betrayed my expectations in a good way."

This sudden praise left Allan wiping tears with his apron.

"Well, I've been blessed with good friends…and a great master," he admitted, pointing in Lloyd's direction.

"Lloyd, I must thank you once again," Threonine said. "Please train my idiot son well."

"I-I'm not teaching him anything important!" Lloyd spluttered. "But honestly, Allan's doing really well and picks up on things fast, so I'm sure he'll be standing on his own two feet in no time!"

"Well, if you say so, I'm sure that's true! Good news, eh, Allan?"

"L-Lloyd…I've done nothing to earn your praise…"

Lloyd, of course, was talking about *cooking*. Blissfully unaware of this, Allan sobbed into his apron.

"Didn't expect anyone to cry after being told they can stand on their own in the kitchen," Lloyd said, confused.

Selen's father had been watching all this.

"I suspected you weren't the eldest Lidocaine boy," he admitted, totally calm.

Threonine noticed and stepped forward, bowing low. "I apologize for the deception. Lloyd here was a stand-in."

Threonine further elaborated on his apology, as well as the reason why a proxy had been necessary.

Selen's father showed no signs of anger—in fact, he almost smiled.

"No, that's all fine. I should never have forced a marriage arrangement without considering my daughter's feelings. And…"

He glanced at his daughter, Selen.

"I'm pleased to have learned how she feels."

"Father…," she breathed.

He looked away, staring at the label on the drink in his hand.

"Oh, this is that thing shy people do whenever they feel awkward, huh?" Riho said. That explained a lot about Selen's father. When he had first seen his daughter's face without the belt, his eyes had immediately dropped to the pamphlet in his hand…and then there were all the times he'd wound up looking at walls or somewhere else entirely.

"You mean…?"

"He was just uncomfortable! He hadn't seen his daughter in a while, so…?" Lloyd prompted.

Selen's father nodded curtly. "I hadn't seen her face in…over a decade. Honestly…I didn't know what to do with myself."

He continued examining the drink label from every angle. Definitely some social anxiety going on there.

"You don't have a shy bone in your body, but your dad totally does."

Riho's sarcasm fell on deaf ears. Selen moved to her father's side.

"Father, I'm going back to Azami. I'm taking school seriously. I'm going to come back a successful soldier."

Hearing her mind made up, Selen's father placed the drink back on the table and bowed his head to Lloyd.

"Lloyd, take care of my daughter."

"No, she's the one helping me! I don't deserve any bowed heads…"

But the cliché her father had let slip was all it took to send Selen back to her usual self.

"Parent approved! Time for us to get married! Married!"

"Seriously, did you inherit *anything* from your father? Like a sense of shame?!"

But in this state, no amount of Riho's spite could stop Selen. And her father smiled, like fathers did when their kids were having fun.

"Ha-ha-ha…I remember when you were little. Always getting in trouble."

"She still is!"

"Hush, Riho."

Selen's father clearly took their bickering as a sign of friendship.

"I should have taken a better look at you. I promise I'll be more of a father and watch how your military career turns out, Selen. Good luck."

"F-Father..."

What a lovely reconciliation.

At this point, one of the border police arrived, looking concerned.

"Er, excuse me... Is there someone named Selen Hemein here?"

"Oh, that's—" Selen started to say.

But before she could, the cop continued, "Apparently, she had a huge order of bottle bombs sent to the hotel. She was already on our watch lists for stalking in Azami... Anyone know her? We'd like to bring her in for voluntary questioning."

There was a long silence.

"...That's the one who went running the second she saw the cops," Selen said. "Headed for the mountains."

"What?! Thank you for telling us!"

The police bowed and ran off in the direction Selen had pointed.

"......"

"Don't look away, Daddy-o," Riho said, patting him on the shoulders.

His smile had gone from warm to the stoic expression of a businessman forced to apologize to a client for a mix-up. He bowed his head low.

"Lloyd...please...take care of my daughter."

"Oh Lord, Father! You already said that! Repeating it can't make Lloyd and me any closer than we already are."

"Selen, this one meant something else *entirely*," Riho explained.

This time, it was definitely along the lines of "supervise and discipline my daughter so her mistakes don't land her in prison." But Selen kept putting her own spin on everything.

While all this was going on, Alka was sitting on a couch in the corner, looking lonely and swinging her legs around.

"Hmm, all that work I did, and Lloyd gets the credit! So sad." It seemed the kid grandma expected more gratitude.

"S-sorry, Chief...I didn't mean to hog the glory...," Lloyd apologized.

This was all part of Alka's plan. Once she got that out of Lloyd, she dramatically exposed her shoulders.

"After all that memory manipulation, I'm just so tired. I *have* to get a massage!"

This was delivered as if she were reading cue cards, but Lloyd failed to notice.

"Oh? Then let me give you one to make up for it!"

"Heh-heh! Those are the words I wanted to hear!"

The kiddy grandma dove face-first into the nearest couch.

"A...a massage? Wait, Lloyd!" Marie yelped.

"Careful! Make sure you do a *proper* massage!" Riho insisted.

Both well aware of the false information Lloyd have been given, both very red-faced as a result.

"Yes, Kikyou taught me how to do a proper massage!"

"Then...fine." Alka paid this no attention, grinning in anticipation.

"Gweh-heh-heh... A proper Lloyd massage... Watch this and weep, riffraff! See the strength of our bond!"

""""" ...What's *that* mean?"""""

Rolling his shoulders in preparation, Lloyd approached Alka.

"Okay, massage time! I only just learned what real massages are yesterday, so I hope this goes all right!"

"A real massage? That sounds intense! How much further will it go? You can't mean..."

Lloyd's arm slipped around Alka's waist.

"Whoo! Hands going places! Your 'real massage' starts down—"

"Here goes nothing!" Lloyd threw her into a back suplex. Perfect form.

There was a light *thunk*, and Alka was left with her legs sticking out into the corridor like a victim of *The Inugami Family*. She moved no more.

"Well, Riho? How was that for a massage?"

"Uh, Lloyd...," Riho said, looking very serious.

"Yes?"

"If you do that to anyone else, you'll get arrested. Never do that again."

"O-oh… What kind of massage do you have to do to escape arrest?!"

Lloyd's cry echoed through the hotel.

Her head jammed in the floor, Alka's legs twitched like those of an insect hit with bug spray.

"What goes around comes around."

"Definitely."

Neither Marie nor Riho had any sympathy for her.

Suppose a villain invented a weapon and lost her life at its hands. It was a fitting end that deserved no pity.

Afterwor

Before writing this work, I was actually writing a story about space.

But as I was combing through research, I realized something.

——The universe is…*really* big.

My core stats are basically on the level of your average armadillo. For me to finish a story about space would take forever, so I put that novel aside.

But the deadline for *GA Bunko* imprint was looming! What was I to do? In that moment, I saw a little note scribbled at the edge of the page: a country villager who was overpowered in the big city…

Since my greatest strength is decisiveness, I knew then that I could write a book based on that concept. Incidentally, my greatest weakness is poor judgment.

Hoping for nothing more than to make people laugh and remember my name, I wrote a book and sent it in.

And that submission was *Suppose a Kid from the Last Dungeon Boonies Moved to a Starter Town.*

Everyone told me it was a really long title, but I never expected to win an award! I just wanted to get noticed. Hence the long title. I never spared a thought for what might happen in later volumes.

I'm very grateful to find myself writing Volume 3.

——My first novel, *Butt-Naked Berserk Shimamura*? I'd thought up five volumes' worth of plot. World annihilation. Storylines where the cter's mind and nether regions are rocked by his personal the views of those around him. A dramatic reveal when his sister discovers his true identity.

Your brother's a butt-naked berserker," Shimamura admits, before his sister for the first time.

guess no one would buy that. Commercially or morally.

any rate, I'm Toshio Satou. The pressure's been getting to me lately, my hair has been falling out, giving me a very punk rock look.

I would like to start with some words of gratitude.

My illustrator, Nao Watanuki—thank you for the beautiful art once again! Selen looks so lovely on the cover, it reminded me she's actually one of the series' heroines.

All my editors, everyone on the business end of things, proofreaders, designers—I can never thank you enough.

To my local dermatologist, thank you for the wonderful medicine. My hair came back! I might start losing it again in three or four months. I suppose we'll meet again then.

And now for some updates.

There's going to be a manga adaption of this series! It's scheduled to start at the end up September in *Gangan GA*.

Hajime Fusemachi will be handling the art. That's the same person who adapted Kazuma Kamachi's all-star novel, *A Certain Magical Heavy Zashiki-Warashi Deals With a Simple Killer Princess' Marriage Circumstances*. Long titles may be a part of their destiny.

I've already seen the roughs, and the artist's care for the story and dialogue is beyond incredible. I'm truly honored. Thank you so much!

...When I was first told about the adaption, my reaction was "Oh?" Like when a discrepancy between a ledger and an account is too large, it actually makes your mind get very calm. Same phenomenon. Like, there must be some mistake. I assumed they'd meant that call for someone else. Until very recently.

When I got sent the roughs, I was so surprised, I fell over. Maybe that's when all my hair fell out. I have the mental fortitude of a sunfish.

Dear readers, I hope you will enjoy seeing the adorable designs Noa Watanuki created brought to life by the hands of Hajime Fusemachi.

I am truly blessed. Even if this costs me my hair, I am satisfied. Every time I take a bow, people will be surprised by the patchy bald spots, but I remain happy.

In conclusion, I'd like to thank every reader who picks up this book.

I would be overjoyed to see you again in Volume 4—and I'm thrilled I can even say that.

Toshio Satou